W9-ALN-091

Listen!

Also by

STEPHANIE S. TOLAN

Welcome to the Ark
Flight of the Raven
Surviving the Applewhites
Ordinary Miracles
Plague Year
Who's There?
The Face in the Mirror
Save Halloween!
A Good Courage

Listen!

STEPHANIE S. TOLAN

HarperCollins*Publishers*

Library of Congress Cataloging-in-Publication
Data is available.
ISBN-10: 0-06-057935-8
ISBN-13: 978-0-06-057935-7
ISBN-10: 0-06-057936-6 (lib. bdg.)
ISBN-13: 978-0-06-057936-4 (lib. bdg.)

Typography by Amy Ryan
1 2 3 4 5 6 7 8 9 10

First Edition

*To Coyote, loving spirit,
and the dogs and people of Eagle Lake
who helped bring him in from the wild*

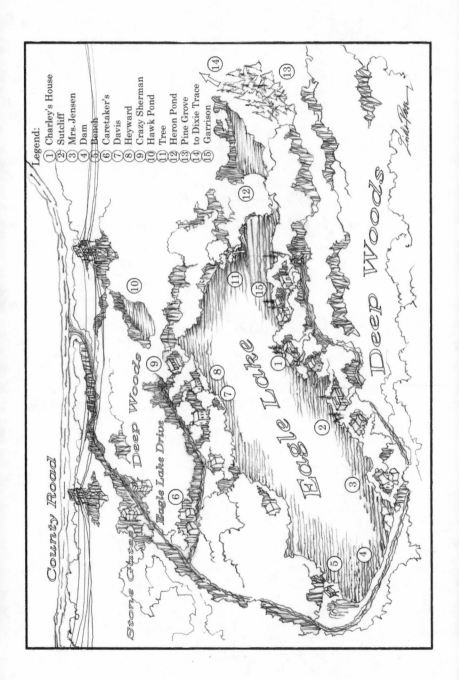

Legend:
1. Charley's House
2. Sutcliff
3. Mrs. Jensen
4. Dam
5. Bench
6. Caretaker's
7. Davis
8. Heyward
9. Crazy Sherman
10. Hawk Pond
11. Tree
12. Heron Pond
13. Pine Grove
14. to Dixie Trace
15. Garrison

County Road

Deep Woods

Stone Gates

Eagle Lake Drive

Eagle Lake

Deep Woods

Listen!

Dog

Charley is halfway across the dam, sweat dripping down her back under her T-shirt, when her father drives past her on his way back to work. She doesn't look at him. As slowly as he is driving, the car still kicks up gray-white dust from the gravel road. She walks through the dust, as straight and tall as she can make herself, jamming her walking stick into the stones as she goes, trying not to limp. She is walking. It is what he wants, and she is doing it. But if he's so interested in the best thing for her, why can't he let her decide what that is?

"I won't have you sitting in that chair all summer!" he yelled when she refused to come sit with him and eat the lunch Sarita had to scramble to fix when he showed up suddenly, unexpectedly, in the middle of the workday.

"Summer hasn't even started yet," she yelled back.

"It's the last day of school—for kids who are *in* school," he said.

You'd think it was her fault that she isn't in school, finishing the sixth grade with everybody else!

"You only have ten weeks to build up your strength and be ready when school starts again. You are to get outside today. It's time, Charlene! Your physical therapist says you're healing well and a little exercise is all you need to get back to normal. You will start by walking. Today. Is that clear?" He was using his I-am-the-boss voice that keeps a factory full of workers in line.

She lowered the footrest of the recliner chair, picked up her walking stick from the floor, and got to her feet as gracefully as she could. Without a word she went down the hall to her room and put on her sneakers. Then, pounding the stick on the floor as she went, she walked straight through the living room and the dining room, out the sliding glass door, and down the ramp he had had built over the stairs her second week in the hospital.

Her father was at the breakfast table in the lake room when she left, waving his fork in the air as he talked into his cell phone. He might have taken time to come home for lunch, but he hadn't really left his work, Charley thinks as his car moves up the hill on the other side of the dam and disappears around the curve. It's what her father does—work. *Normal* for him means his eighty-hour workweek.

By the time the dust from his car settles, Charley has reached the end of the dam, where there is a bench under a willow tree by the water. She could sit there in the shade awhile, looking at Eagle Lake, its ripples glittering in the sun. She could rest her leg and then go home again. But she keeps walking, up the slope of the road.

She can walk all right. She is done with the wheelchair. Done with crutches. The "miracle" of the rod the doctors stuck into the bone in her right leg from her hip to her knee means she has never had to wear a cast. By now all there is to show for what happened to her is the scar down her leg where they put the rod in. And the walking stick she made so she wouldn't have to use the stupid old-lady-looking cane Tony, her physical terrorist, tried to give her after the crutches.

Her father wants her back to normal. Normal. What is that? Is that what her life was the first week in March? Before her friend Amy's brother Travis gave them a ride home from school that rainy Monday afternoon? Before he got to showing off and playing NASCAR driver? Before what the papers called a "one-car accident" that was really one car and one tree? She can't remember the accident that put her in the hospital and ended the school year for her. She can't even remember the first few days after it. The doctors say, because of the concussion, she probably never will.

If there is one thing she's learned for sure in her twelve years of life, it is that you can't go back to the way things used to be. No matter how much you want to. You can't go back. Somehow or other, you have to keep going forward. It's just that she hasn't figured out yet how to do that.

Whether she spends the whole summer in the recliner chair or out here walking the hot, dusty road around Eagle Lake, it can't be like the last two summers. This summer can't be Charley and Amy at Amy's house swimming in Amy's pool, playing tennis, going to movies, hanging out at the mall, spending whole days at a time at Carrowinds amusement park with Amy's family. Because this summer Travis is working to pay his father back for the car he wrecked. And Amy . . . Amy . . .

Charley stabs her walking stick into the gravel, and a little puff of dust rises into the air.

She has reached the split where the gravel road that is Eagle Lake Drive goes straight ahead, past the caretaker's house and out to the paved county road, and also right, through the woods toward the south side of the lake. She turns right and keeps walking. Where the road splits again—right to the four houses closest to the dam and left to the rest of the houses on the south side of the lake—she goes left. Trees nearly meet over her head—thick woods on one side, woods with houses on the other.

She goes on stabbing her walking stick into the gravel, goes on making the little puffs of dust. Amy, her best friend since second grade, is going off to spend the whole summer at Lake George in upstate New York with Becky Sue Lindner. Charley still can't quite believe it. If it was Amy who'd been smashed up in a car accident, if it was Charley whose brother caused that accident, and if Amy was supposed to be getting out and starting to do stuff to get her strength back, Charley would be right there doing stuff with her. That's what best friends are for.

"Evelyn Lindner was a tennis champion, you know," Amy's mother explained when she called a couple weeks ago to break the news. As if it was her mother, instead of Amy, who had made the decision. "She coaches Becky Sue, and she's offered to coach Amy, too. It's a chance of a lifetime." Amy's mother didn't say that Charley wouldn't be up to playing tennis with Amy this summer. She didn't have to.

Amy called, then, to say it was all her mother's idea,

and she didn't want to go. But Charley knows better. She's seen Amy get what she wants plenty of times before. As soon as Amy's mother said good-bye, Charley hung up, opened her laptop, and deleted every single photo of the two of them together. And she quit responding to Amy's instant messages. Whenever Amy called after that, Charley told Sarita she didn't want to talk.

She won't have to think about calls or e-mails or instant messages from Amy much longer now. The Lindners don't let their kids have computers at Lake George. Today, June 10, is the last day of school, and tomorrow Amy and Becky Sue's family will leave first thing in the morning. They won't be back until the weekend before school starts again.

A hawk screams overhead. Charley stops in the middle of the road and looks up, catching sight of it for only a few seconds before it circles out of sight behind the trees. What does a hawk have to scream about? she thinks. It's up there, riding the air, high and easy, not even moving its wings.

She wipes the sweat from her eyes with her free hand and curses. Her other hand is practically paralyzed from holding onto her walking stick so hard. She understands now why canes are made the way they are—so you can put your weight on the handle. All those hours she spent whittling the bark off her stick and smoothing it, carving her initials into it, and she'd be better off with the cane Tony wanted to give her.

Now that she has stopped, Charley is suddenly aware of how much her bad leg hurts. Even her so-called good leg aches from the walking. Her jaw hurts, too. She must have been clenching her teeth against the pain, she thinks. What she wants, right this minute, is to be back home, back in the recliner chair with something cold to drink. Right now!

The trouble is she has walked so far that she is almost directly across the lake from her house. Getting home means either turning around and going back the way she came, or walking the woods trail around the shallow end of the lake where there are no houses. The woods trail is shorter. But she doesn't walk the woods trail. Not ever. The woods trail is part of the reason she hates living at Eagle Lake. It's part of the way things used to be, when things really were normal, before the accident and before . . .

Charley stops herself. The woods trail is part of what she will never have back again. Besides, it's tough going, winding steeply up and down, skirting the ridge above the water. Her leg hurts way too much to go that way, even if she wanted to.

She stands in the sticky North Carolina June afternoon, wishing she could fly like that hawk. She will have to turn back and go the long way. At least there's the bench by the dam where she can rest. She will not do this walk again anytime soon, that she knows for sure.

She pulls her soggy T-shirt away from her skin, wipes the sweat off her face again, and turns to start back. That is when she sees the dog.

It is sitting tall and rock still on a smooth patch of bare red dirt at the base of a big sweet gum tree in the woods, barely visible between the scrubby bushes and the tangle of honeysuckle vine that edge the road. It is red-gold, almost the color of the ground it is sitting on, its head high, its dark ears pricked sharply in her direction. The dog's eyes, dark in a narrow, golden face, are looking directly at her. She feels a kind of tremor, as if an electric shock has passed from the dog to her and back again.

She knows all the Eagle Lake dogs. This isn't one of them. For that matter, it doesn't really look like a dog. Not like someone's pet. There's a wildness about it, like a wolf. Or a coyote. It is beautiful. It has a coyote's pointed ears, a black muzzle, and those electrifying eyes. For just a moment there is nothing in all the world except Charley and the dog.

She remembers, then, a dog she saw in the winter, February maybe, scrounging around the Dumpster up past Eagle Lake's stone gates, near the power lines. That dog was about the same size as this one, a dirty reddish color. That dog wasn't beautiful. It had looked wild, though—wild and wary—its shoulders hunched, its ears back, its tail down as it scuttled off into the woods.

Surely this can't be that dog. It couldn't have lived on its own in the woods all these months. She blinks. The dog has vanished. The patch of bare ground where it was sitting is empty now. She can't remember looking away, but she must have. Because the dog is gone. Like a ghost. Just gone.

2

Promise

She is standing there, trying to figure out where the dog is, how it could have gone without a sound, without her seeing it go, when she hears a car coming up the slope of the road behind her. That probably explains the dog's leaving, she thinks. Its sharp ears must have heard the crunch of tires on gravel long before she did.

A black SUV appears over the crest of the hill. It is Mrs. Davis with her kids, Jeremy and Bethanne, and Sadie, their golden retriever. The car comes on past their drive and stops beside her.

Mrs. Davis puts down her window. "Hey, Charley! You're looking great! A little hot—but great. This your first time around the lake?"

Charley nods.

"Good for you!"

The back window goes down, and Bethanne puts her head out. "Are you all done with your crutches?"

"All done." Charley says to Mrs. Davis, "Have you all seen a wild dog hanging around?"

"You mean Wolfie?" Bethanne says.

Mrs. Davis laughs. "Have we seen him? He's Sadie's best friend—follows her everywhere she goes. He showed up about a month ago, and he's been hanging around ever since. That dog's a real sweetie, if you ask me, except he's terrified of people. Something really bad must have happened to him."

In spite of the heat, Charley feels goose bumps rise on her arms. *Something really bad.* "How does he eat?" she asks.

"Doesn't much, as far as I know. He's thin as a rail."

"He's practically starving. But Mommy won't let us feed him," Bethanne says.

Mrs. Davis shrugs. "You feed a dog and you're stuck with it. Sadie's more than enough dog for us. Somebody around here must be giving him something, though. I can't believe he's living entirely on mice and voles."

"He could catch squirrels," Jeremy says, sticking his

blond head out the window next to Bethanne. "There's bazillions of squirrels."

"Too many trees," Mrs. Davis tells him. "It's too easy for them to get away." She turns back to Charley. "I called Animal Control—thought maybe if they took him, somebody might adopt him. They couldn't catch him. That dog's too wily. They baited the trap with a can of tuna—told us tuna'd catch any dog. Not that one. They said they'd come back when they could gather up enough volunteers to surround him, but it's been weeks and I haven't heard anything."

Charley thinks about a dog too wily to be caught like other dogs. A starving dog that something really bad happened to. She imagines the golden dog with the wild eyes surrounded by people closing in to catch him and put him in a cage. It makes her feel sick to her stomach. "Maybe I could get him to come live with us."

As soon as the words are out of her mouth, she wants to take them back. She's never had a dog. She knows nothing about dogs.

Mrs. Davis grins. "That would be super! We've been worried to death about him."

"Can't nobody get close to him," Jeremy says. "We been trying. How're y'all even going to get him over to the other side of the lake?"

Charley doesn't have an answer. It isn't as if she's thought this out.

"Well, good luck to you," Mrs. Davis says, and begins to back the car down the road. "Anything we can do to help, just let us know."

Charley stands there feeling like an idiot. She doesn't want a dog. Not any dog, let alone a wild and terrified one.

Except there was that moment when she first saw him. Maybe it was the way he was sitting, so straight and tall, so incredibly alert. Right then he didn't look scared or starving. He looked . . . wild. Magical. Part of the woods.

When Jeremy and Bethanne get out of the car in their driveway, Sadie leaps out between them and tears down the road toward Charley. She jumps up and puts both paws on Charley's chest so that Charley has to hang on to her walking stick to keep from being knocked over. Sadie's tongue slathers Charley's face.

"Down, Sadie!" Mrs. Davis yells. "Get down! Charley's in no shape to have dogs jumping on her."

"It's okay." Charley pushes Sadie down and wipes her cheek on the shoulder of her T-shirt. The wild dog is suddenly there, as if he has materialized out of the woods. Like a ghost, Charley thinks again. Sadie runs to greet him. Tails wagging, they touch noses and then jump at each other. The wild dog is very nearly the same color as Sadie, except for his black muzzle and ears, and very nearly the same size. Charley can see his ribs through his fur, and his tail is matted. If it were combed, Charley thinks, it would be every bit as thick and plumy as Sadie's.

Sadie begins chasing him around a hydrangea bush in the Davises' yard. The wild dog swerves and cuts behind a tree, leaping out as Sadie runs past and grabbing her by the scruff of the neck. Bigger and heavier, Sadie knocks him sideways and breaks his grip, then grabs him by one ear.

"I told you they were best friends," Mrs. Davis says, pulling a bag of groceries out of the back end of her car. "Come help, kids!"

Charley thinks about what Mrs. Davis said about the wild dog following Sadie. "Do you think if Sadie came around the lake with me, he would follow us?"

"I wouldn't be surprised. He follows when Don takes Sadie running. He doesn't like the road, though. It's too wide. Too exposed, I think. He likes to stay under cover in the woods."

Not the road. If she tries this, walking Sadie to get the wild dog to follow, she'll *have* to take the woods trail. No. She won't do that.

But the dog is starving. Again her mouth seems to work without her permission, as if somebody else is using it. "Would it be okay, then, if I walked Sadie over to my house? If the dog follows, I could feed him something."

"Good idea." Mrs. Davis reaches into her grocery bag and pulls out a can of dog food. She gives it to Jeremy to take to Charley. "Give him that."

"Thanks." Charley puts the can of dog food into the pocket of her cargo shorts.

"Good luck!" Mrs. Davis starts for the house. "When we want Sadie home," she calls over her shoulder, "we'll just holler for her. She can swim back."

"Can I go along with Charley?" Bethanne asks.

"You may not! That dog doesn't need any extra people to contend with. Bring the milk!"

When Mrs. Davis and the children go into the house, Charley calls to Sadie, "You want to go for a walk?"

Before she has a chance to fend the dog off with her walking stick, there are new red-orange paw prints on the front of her shirt.

Charley looks for the wild dog and sees that he's back in the woods across the road. "I'm not making any promises," she tells the dog. "Except this one. If you come around the lake with Sadie and me now, I'll give you some food. That's all." A slant of sunlight through the trees catches the gold of his fur, and he twitches his ears. But he doesn't move.

"Let's go," Charley calls to Sadie. "Let's walk!"

Sadie barks and runs ahead toward where the road ends at the kudzu-covered slope down to the power line right-of-way. Charley uses the bottom of her T-shirt to wipe the sweat from her face, and starts limping after her. As if she understands the plan, Sadie turns onto the narrow trail that winds down the steep hill next to the last house on the south side of the lake, Crazy Sherman's log cabin, with its odd collection of sculptures made from bits of rusted junk.

Limping, Charley follows. At first she is glad to get off the road, where walking on the gravel keeps twisting her ankle and knee, sending jolts of pain through her leg. But the trail, narrow and uneven underfoot, isn't much better. It is crisscrossed with kudzu vines, like an obstacle course of trip wires.

Halfway down she turns to see if the wild dog is following, and her foot catches on a vine. She has to grab for a sapling and stab her stick into the dirt to keep from falling down the hill.

As she pulls herself upright, she catches a glimpse of the wild dog slipping in between the trees up near the road. He is following.

3
The Woods Trail

Gritting her teeth against the pain and keeping her walking stick ahead of her to slow her progress, Charley manages to get down the rest of the hill. At the bottom the trail levels out and crosses the embankment that separates Hawk Pond, the first of two feeder ponds, from the lake.

The trail here is easy walking compared to the hill Charley has just come down and the even steeper hill she'll have to climb on the other side. She is just thinking how grateful she is for this when she notices that the greenery crowding the trail on both sides is dark and shiny and three-leaved. Someone has been keeping the trail open, but just barely. Poison ivy is pushing in toward her bare arms and legs.

There's more poison ivy out here than kudzu and barbed-wire vine and honeysuckle put together.

Charley catches her breath and stops. No. She does not want this voice, this clear and unmistakable voice, in her head. This is what she has been afraid of, why she doesn't walk this trail.

It is too late not to have heard it. She is here at the wild end of the lake, right in the middle of her mother's world. Here, where her mother used to come day after day, season after season, year after year, to take the nature photographs that made her famous—the photographs that eventually took her away forever. Charley shakes her head, as if she can shake memory away.

Focus, she tells herself firmly. Pay attention to this moment, to the reason you are here. Nothing else. Since the day her father, his face gray, turned from the telephone to tell her about the plane crash in the Brazilian rainforest, Charley has worked at closing down the past. She has gotten very good at it.

Ahead of her, Sadie is standing chest deep in the pond, drinking. Charley looks around for the wild dog. He is nowhere to be seen. This is crazy, she thinks. Just crazy. If it weren't for the wild dog, she would never have come here, stirred up memories, raised her mother's voice in her mind. She swallows hard a couple of times around the sharpness in her throat, and then begins moving carefully forward, concentrating on staying in the very middle of the trail, using her walking stick to fend off the poison ivy that seems to be reaching out at her. She will have to remember to wash really well when she gets home and hope for the best.

When she reaches the end of the ivy patch, she crosses the water trickling into a foot-wide crack in the old concrete spillway between pond and lake, and stands for a moment facing the hill ahead of her. She needs to rest before tackling it. A tree has fallen into the pond, dragging up a mass of red dirt where its roots broke free of the hillside. The roots reach out toward the trail. She grabs one and pulls herself up the first steep rise, pushing with her stick. Then she manages to clamber onto the wide trunk that stretches like a bench toward the water and she sits, aware of the throbbing in her leg, doing her best to keep her mind on this moment.

It is no good. She is looking across the water as her mother used to, camera poised, waiting for a heron to come stalking through the reeds, a kingfisher to settle on a branch over the water, or the pond's resident muskrat to come out of his den beneath the embankment. Even now a photograph of that muskrat, nose barely breaking the water's surface, early sunlight glinting on the ripples that v out behind, hangs on the wall of the lake room. The day of the funeral, Charley took every single one of her mother's photographs down from the walls of her room. But her father left others up all over the house. She has learned to live among them without seeing them.

She shifts her gaze away from the pond and sees the wild dog at the other side of the poison ivy patch, about to come through. He catches her looking at him and stops. He looks like what he is—a starving, frightened, probably abused dog. There is nothing beautiful, nothing magical about him. What has she been thinking?

Sadie comes up out of the pond, shakes water all over Charley. Then she runs back through the ivy to pounce on the wild dog. The two of them tussle briefly, and Sadie comes running back.

The wild dog doesn't come with her. He is standing up the far hill now, sheltered by the trees. Charley remembers she has promised him food. She doesn't break promises. Anyway, she is already here, has already shaken the memories loose. She will rest till her leg is ready to climb this hill, and then she will keep her concentration carefully on each step she takes all the way home. She can. She will.

Sadie has already gone ahead up the trail. "Come on!" she calls to the wild dog. At the sound of her voice, he vanishes into the shadows again. If this dog can't stand her looking at him, can't stand the sound of her voice, Charley thinks, she won't be able to save him anyway, won't be able to give him a home.

"Suit yourself!" she yells at him. I don't want him, she tells herself as she slides off the fallen tree and starts up the hill. This is the steepest part of the trail, more cliff than hill, in spite of the trees and shrubs growing from between the rocks. She has to use both hands here, one for her walking stick, the other to hold onto saplings, roots, branches—anything to drag herself upward and keep her from slipping back.

When the trail levels off along a ridge about two thirds of the way up the hill, the walking becomes easier again. Possible, at least. She has just managed to get over a gully that has carved a nearly three-foot gap in the trail when she looks up and sees a tree, leaning low over the path. The Limbo Tree.

She stops, her mother's voice in her head again. *Jack be limbo, Jack be quick, Jack jump over limbo stick.* She can almost see her mother now, setting her equipment on the ground, bending backward, doing the limbo under the tree. Memory rushes in—herself so little she could walk upright under this tree. And then the day she discovered she'd grown enough to have to bend herself backward the way her mother did. The day her mother took a picture of her doing the limbo for the first time.

Charley shakes her head again. Nothing but a downed tree, she tells herself. One of hundreds of trees Hurricane Hugo and its tornadoes toppled all around Eagle Lake. It's just one that happened to get its topmost branches caught among the standing trees so that it didn't fall all the way to the ground. That's all.

The tree is leaning closer to the ground than she remembers. Or maybe in these two years she has grown that much taller. Its bark is falling off in chunks, and the tree itself is disintegrating. There are bits of dark, rotted wood littering the trail.

Sadie comes thundering back down the trail as if she wants to know why Charley has stopped. "I'm coming, I'm coming," Charley tells her. Then, slowly and deliberately, she bends forward—forward, not back—to duck under the tree.

4
Feeding

Twice more along the trail, Charley has to stop and rest, once on a boulder and the other time on a tree stump. She hasn't seen the wild dog since Hawk Pond, she thinks as she sits on the stump. So she's been saved from herself. She doesn't have to keep her promise if he doesn't come with her to get fed. Sadie can swim home, and Charley will take the can of dog food back to Mrs. Davis the next time (weeks and weeks from now) she feels like walking all the way around the lake.

No sooner has she thought this than she catches a glimpse of movement and sees a red-gold form slip quickly across the trail back along the ridge she has just walked. If she hadn't stopped to rest, she'd never have known he was still there. Somehow he can move through the woods with no sound at all.

Sadie is another story, charging around in the dead leaves, splashing into the water to take a swim when the trail winds down near the lake, coming back to shake on Charley, then rolling on the ground to dry herself. Charley could have closed her eyes anytime on the walk and known exactly where Sadie was. Besides that, no raccoon or muskrat, no fox or beaver with half a brain would show its face within a mile of Sadie.

This is why she has never had a dog. Nature photography requires patience and stillness. Quiet. Nothing chasing animals away.

But there is no one doing nature photography anymore. She can have a dog now if she wants.

When she and Sadie come down out of the woods and cross the embankment at Heron Pond, the smaller of the two ponds, half-choked with cattails, Charley hasn't seen the wild dog again. But she knows now that not seeing him doesn't mean that he isn't around somewhere, among the trees, keeping pace with them.

She is picking her way across the Heron Pond spillway on broken chunks of concrete, listening to the cheerful sound of the waterfall where the water slides over a tumble of boulders on its way to the lake, when Sadie runs past her, splashing her with mud and water. It feels so good on her hot, sticky skin that she wishes she could climb down and sit under the waterfall, letting it wash away the sweat and grime. What she wants more, though, is to get home, wash the poison ivy off, take a pain pill, and lie down for a while.

At last she emerges from among the trees onto the broad swathe of trail that is the sewer line access for the housing developments up beyond the woods that surround Eagle Lake. Every couple of years the utilities people come with a truck and mow down the poison ivy and blackberry brambles, the honeysuckle and sweet gum saplings that grow so fast and thick that they practically choke off the trail between cuttings. She follows it across a tiny creek and up the last slope to the chain that stretches across the end of Eagle Lake Drive. The chain is low enough to step over.

Jasmine and Bernie, the two German shepherds who live at the last house on the north side of the lake, bark at Sadie from their pen down near the water as she goes by. Sadie stays well away. Jasmine, the younger shepherd, sometimes attacks other female dogs, so Mr. Garrison, their owner, keeps them penned while he's at work.

When Charley gets home, Sadie is with her, but the wild dog is not. As she starts down the driveway toward the house, she hears Jasmine and Bernie barking again. A minute later the wild dog comes down the road, shoulders hunched, nose up, sniffing for danger. He really does look like a coyote, Charley thinks. Rangy and wild. As she watches him, braving the open road to follow them, his eyes meet hers for a moment. Again there is that feeling like an electrical current between them. *Coyote.* She thinks the word toward him as if she were saying it out loud. *That's your name. Coyote.*

She makes her way down the driveway, up the ramp, and through the sliding door into the dining room. The vacuum cleaner is running in her father's bedroom. Sarita, her eternal jigsaw puzzle abandoned on its table by the windows overlooking the lake, is working. "Sarita!" she yells, not sure she can be heard. "I'm back."

The vacuum stops. "You okay?"

"Yeah!" It isn't true, but as long as she isn't actually dead, she's okay enough for Sarita. Charley figures she's just another chore for this woman her father pays to run the household. Like the laundry or a room that needs vacuuming.

She takes the can of dog food into the kitchen and opens it, then gets out a heavy serving bowl. Hurrying, she spoons out the food—cube-shaped chunks of meat with gravy—and goes to see if the dog is still out there. If Sadie starts for home, Coyote will surely follow her. It takes her a minute to spot him across the road, almost in the woods, standing and watching the house.

She sets the bowl on the buffet and opens the sliding door. Then, stick in one hand, bowl in the other, she steps out onto the ramp. Instantly the dog disappears into the woods. Charley can hear Sadie swimming for home, making big splashes with her front paws the way she always does. "Lunchtime!" Charley calls to the wild dog she can't see anymore. "Come and get it!"

She limps out to the end of the drive and sets the bowl down where the cement meets the gravel. "Lunchtime!" she calls again. Charley steps back from the food and waits for the dog to come out. He doesn't. So she turns around and goes back to the house. When she gets to the ramp, she turns to watch. Still the dog doesn't come out. Finally she goes all the way back inside and closes the sliding door. She moves to the dining room window to watch.

Sarita, tall and lean as a heron in her faded blue jeans and navy T-shirt, comes down the hall from the bedroom. "What's up?"

There is no way to know what Sarita would think of having a dog in the house. She is as communicative as a statue. But it isn't Sarita Charley has to convince; it is her father. Charley motions Sarita to the narrow window by the front door. "Watch. Out on the drive."

The dog comes out of the woods and stands for a moment looking toward the house. Then he crouches low to the ground and begins to creep up on the food dish, as if it might be booby-trapped. He sniffs at it quickly, then backs away. He looks to his right, his left, and over his shoulder, sniffs again, then begins creeping forward, his tail tightly tucked between his legs. He wants the food, Charley can see. Really wants it. But he seems terrified of it, too.

Finally, standing as far back from the bowl as he possibly can, he stretches his neck to reach the food. He wolfs a couple of bites and then backs up to check all around again, muscles tensed and ready to run.

"That's the stray from the other side of the lake," Sarita says.

"How'd you know about him?"

"Saw him a couple of times up by the mailboxes. Scooted off when he saw me, though. Scruffy-lookin' thing."

The dog goes on eating, gulping quickly, stopping every couple of mouthfuls to check for danger. When he finishes, he slips back into the woods.

"Mrs. Davis says nobody can get near that dog," Sarita says.

"Nobody can."

"So how come you're feeding him?"

"Because he's hungry." It is more than that, she knows. But Charley can't explain it even to herself. "I'm thinking maybe he could come live with us."

"Huh!" Sarita says, and runs a hand over her fine frizz of gray hair. "What's your father going to say?"

"I don't know." Whatever he says, Charley thinks, surprised at how strongly she feels, suddenly, she will find a way to have this dog in her life.

5

Night

*C*harley is in bed, watching television, when her father gets home and comes to her room to say good night. "You don't know anything about training dogs," he says when she asks him about Coyote. "Taming a wild one is no way to start. You have no idea what's happened to that dog, what scars he has. A professional trainer probably couldn't turn a dog like that into a pet."

He doesn't understand, Charley thinks. She isn't exactly sure she does. She wants Coyote in her life, but she does *not* want a pet.

"If you really want a dog, we could get you a puppy, an animal that doesn't have any history to overcome. Even that wouldn't be easy. A puppy needs lots of attention." Her father leans against her doorframe and frowns. His face is thinner than it used to be. And less certain. "On the other hand, training a pup would give you something to do this summer, something to focus on and get you out of the house—if you think you're up to it. We'd have to get some dog training books—"

"I don't want a puppy!" Charley says. "I want this dog. If he doesn't come live with us, he's going to die. Whether he dies in the woods or at the shelter, he's going to die." There is no point trying to explain the connection she feels with this dog.

Paul Morgan loosens his tie and sighs. Death is not a subject they talk about. Charley crosses her arms on her chest and looks him straight in the eye. "*This* dog will give me something to do this summer, too."

She watches his face change. He has made up his mind. "All right. But if he shows the slightest sign of being dangerous, the deal's off."

"Mrs. Davis says he's a sweetie. She's right. You can see it in his eyes. He's just scared of people."

"A scared dog is a dangerous dog."

"How could he be dangerous? He won't come close enough to a human being to bite."

"You really think you can tame him?"

"Yes." Charley puts more certainty in her voice than she feels. "Feeding him is a start."

Her father becomes all business now, settling into the mode that makes him most comfortable. "All right, then. You and Sarita can go pick up some supplies tomorrow. Training books. Food. Dish. Collar. Leash." He ticks them off on his fingers.

Charley thinks about the golden dog on a leash. "I don't think we need a leash yet."

"Collar and leash," he says again. "You're going to need a way to control him."

She doesn't argue.

Her father comes over to kiss the top of her head and leaves her thinking about a dog who disappears into the woods when she so much as looks at him. Even so, she feels her heart lift. She turns off the television and the light over her bed and slides down under the covers. "Coyote," she whispers. Where is he right now? She closes her eyes and an image comes into her mind of the dog, a pale shape in the darkness, curled on the flat, smooth ground of his place by the sweet gum tree across the lake. His nose is tucked under his tail. The woods are silent around him. As he has been every night for as long as he can remember, he is alone. But tonight he is not hungry. He sighs in his sleep, and Charley imagines him dreaming of the golden retriever he plays with every day. And of the human who fed him.

It is pitch-black when Charley wakes from the nightmare, breathing hard. For a moment she thinks she is back in the hospital. But it is too dark for that. Home, then. Her own room. She hopes she didn't scream.

Dad hates it when she wakes him in the night. He never knows what to do, what to say. Once, a long time ago now—back near the beginning—she thought she saw the shine of tears on his cheeks as he sat on the edge of her bed, patting her awkwardly, and she felt herself go cold all over. She needs him not to cry. Never to cry. "Only a dream," he was saying. "Only a dream." She knew as well as he did that there were worse things than dreams.

When she had the nightmare in the hospital, the nurses stopped coming when she screamed, it happened so often. It wasn't worth interrupting whatever else they were doing at that hour. She checks her alarm clock. Three eighteen, the glowing numbers say.

She puts her hands on her belly and takes a long, slow breath, feeling her belly rise as she breathes. Then she counts to four as she lets the air out slowly, steadily. She does this again, three times, four times. It is the most useful thing Tony the physical terrorist taught her. The breathing smoothes out the sharp edges of panic whenever the nightmare comes. It works. Always. What it doesn't do is keep the nightmare from coming back. Familiar as it is by now, every time feels like the first time. And real—absolutely real. There is no way to know it is a dream until the panic shoves her up and out of sleep.

She is running through a huge, bright, indoor place, full of people dragging suitcases, carrying boxes or small children. It has to be an airport, but not Charlotte/Douglas. There is nothing she recognizes. It is full of carts that beep and beep to move people out of the way as they roar past. She keeps having to dodge the carts, every one full of people who glare at her as if she shouldn't be there. Lots of them are kids from school. Amy is on one of the carts, looking the other way, holding a backpack. Charley calls out, but when the girl turns around she isn't Amy anymore.

Charley is looking for someone, but she doesn't know who. She is filled with the sense that she has to, *has to* find this person. There is much more to the dream, things she can never remember clearly when she wakes up—a feeling of hours passing, moving in and out of rooms or stores or landscapes, trying to find the place she is supposed to be, the person she needs to meet, getting more and more desperate. It is feelings, not images, she remembers. But there is always one thing that comes with her clearly into waking. She can always remember what it was that made her scream, that woke her up.

A spot suddenly appears in front of her in the air. It isn't very big at first, just a black polka dot hovering in front of her. But then it starts to grow, as if a hole is opening up in the world. There is a terrible sound, a kind of roaring, shrieking sound, as the black spot gets bigger and bigger, comes closer and closer. She can see that it is infinitely deep, a swirling blackness that is somehow alive, that wants to swallow her up.

Charley doesn't remember the first days in the hospital, doesn't know for sure it was this nightmare she had there right after the accident. But the nurses told her about the screaming. So it must have been. It's the dream she's been having for two years. It just happened more often in the hospital.

Charley pulls the sheet up under her chin and breathes slowly, counting. Memory, she thinks, is a mysterious thing. Dreams can fade, like the way in the summer there'll be a wet spot in the road up ahead that disappears as you get close. But until the accident, she thought real life was solid. Things that really happened were there, impossible to forget, like massive boulders that you had to work and work and work to move.

Sarita says her father went nearly nuts the first days Charley was in the hospital, because every time Charley fell asleep it was like turning off a computer without saving. Her memory would get wiped clean. "Where am I?" she'd ask. "What happened?" Just like in the movies. And her father would have to tell her the whole story all over again. Eventually he got so tired of telling it that he wrote it down and just handed her the paper to read. With a head injury like that she was lucky, the nurses told her, to be able to read.

That was the first week in March. A whole piece of her life, her real life, is still missing, like a faded dream. It isn't fair, she thinks, blinking into the darkness of her room. It isn't fair that she can't choose what gets wiped clean. It isn't fair that memories so clear they seem real can come crashing in on her without warning, memories that hurt so much she doesn't want them ever, ever again.

She kicks off the covers and sits up on the edge of the bed. The dull ache in her leg has turned into real pain. It is a long time since it has hurt this much in the night when there isn't any weight on it. She walked too much today—yesterday now. She turns on the light, waits till her eyes adjust to the glare, grabs her walking stick, and stands up. Pain or no pain, she has to pee.

While she is in the bathroom she takes a pain pill,

hoping it will help her go back to sleep. Otherwise, she might not be able to. Most times the nightmare throws her out of sleep and leaves her stranded like a whale on a beach.

She gets back into bed, closes her eyes, and lies very still, willing sleep to come. Memories come instead, memories from when she was little. No! She begins to count breaths again, concentrating on the feel of the air going in and out of her nostrils, on the numbers, one—two—three—four. One—two—

Then, against the spangly dark behind her eyelids, the wild dog appears, sitting in a splash of sunlight next to a tree, ears up, dark eyes looking at her.

—three—four—one—two— And Charley is asleep.

6
The Taming

Charley marks a big red 2 on her calendar for this day, June 11. She intends to keep track of this process she has named "The Taming." She writes the words beneath June on the calendar because she hopes it will be finished by the end of the month. That'll be nineteen days, very nearly three weeks. She plans to use food and treats to win him over. Every single one of the Eagle Lake dogs comes willingly to get a treat, even Bo, Mrs. Jensen's black Lab, who is eighteen years old now and has trouble hearing. Lots of the people at the lake take treats for the dogs when they go for a walk, even if they don't have a dog themselves.

Wild and frightened as Coyote is, Charley thinks, he is still a dog. Dogs and people go together. By the end of the month, she wants him in her room at night instead of alone in the woods. Whatever people might have done to him before, she'll prove to him she's different.

After breakfast Charley forces herself to get into Sarita's beat-up old Civic for the drive to the pet store. She still hates getting into cars, hates knowing what awful thing can happen in a car on any ordinary day on any ordinary road. The store is a huge place with whole aisles full of jewel-studded collars and stuffed squeaky toys and even boots and hats and matching jackets. A sign at the front of the store says, "*The* Place for Pets and Their Parents." Parents. So stupid! This is why Charley doesn't want Coyote to be a pet.

Before Paul Morgan left for work, he gave Sarita the rules for this shopping trip, and she walks beside the shopping buggy that Charley is using like a walker, nodding or shaking her head as Charley finds things to put in it. "Dry food only!" she says when Charley stops by the brand of canned food Mrs. Davis gives Sadie. "Your father says if the dog is starving, he'll appreciate anything he gets, and there's no need to spend a fortune."

Charley sighs and moves on toward the aisle with the dry food. She tries to tell from Sarita's expression what she thinks of giving Coyote only dry food. But Sarita's face could be a mahogany mask, it is so still and steady.

She knows the woman must have opinions of her own—
she's too tough not to—but most of the time it's impossible to know what they are. When Sarita doesn't agree
with one of Paul Morgan's orders, her mouth might
twitch a little and something might flash in her eyes. But
nothing more. She's exactly the kind of live-in house-
keeper/babysitter any father would want when he is suddenly left to raise a daughter on his own. He writes her
paycheck, and she does and says whatever he wants her
to. Charley pulls a ten-pound bag of food off a shelf.
Sarita hasn't said what she thinks about The Taming.
Charley doesn't even know if Sarita likes dogs.

Charley chooses two heavy dishes, one for food and
one for water. And a bag of little colored bone-shaped
dog biscuits for treats. She isn't sure what size collar to
get, so she finds a lightweight nylon one that can be
adjusted, and a nylon leash to go with it. She doesn't
expect to use the leash a lot. After all, Coyote will live at
Eagle Lake, where nearly every dog runs free. She
chooses green for collar and leash. Green, she thinks, will
look good against Coyote's red-gold coat.

"Don't forget the training books," Sarita tells her
when she has everything else in the buggy. "Your father
expects you to do this right."

Choosing books takes the longest. There are plenty

to choose from, but none of them seems to have what Charley needs. They're about training, not taming. Finally she picks two, but she doesn't expect them to be much use.

It is afternoon now, and Charley is on the woods trail, on her way to get Sadie and Coyote. She is wearing jeans to keep the poison ivy off and hiking boots to keep her from twisting her ankle and wrenching her knee on the uneven ground. The boots aren't working, and it is very much too hot for jeans.

It would be better to walk earlier in the day, before it gets this hot. But the training books say dogs need routine. Her leg isn't handling the walk today any better than it did yesterday.

It isn't just heat and pain that make the walk miserable this time, though. She must be the first person to come this way today. She keeps walking into lines of spiderweb strung across the trail. They are invisible until the sticky filaments are all over her bare arms, or worse, all over her face. She keeps having to wipe them off her cheeks, her forehead, her hair. Sometimes there are spiders, too—tiny black-and-white spiky, triangular spiders—that drop onto her shoulders and run down her arms. She is just thinking it might be better to walk the long way around on the road—it's too wide for spiderwebs—when she remembers that since she has to walk the dogs on the woods trail, if she doesn't smack into the webs on the way over, she'll just smack into them on the way back.

Spider stick.

It is her mother's voice in her head again. Of course! Her mother used spider sticks to catch webs on the trail. She showed Charley a bush called Russian olive with brittle, easy-to-break branches. Her mother would hold one in front of her as she walked, and the webs would get tangled on the leafy branch, spiders and all. A moment later Charley is walking the trail, safe from webs, peering through the silvery-backed leaves of a spider stick.

She pushes away the memory of walking the trail with her mother and focuses on Coyote. Where is he now? She fills her mind with the image she had of him last night under his tree. "He comes and goes," Mrs. Davis said when Charley called to get permission to keep walking Sadie around the lake every day. The image feels real, it is so clear. He is there, she thinks. He is.

She is wearing a waist pack with supplies for The Taming—dog biscuits and a small makeup mirror. Charley is proud of coming up with this idea—the mirror will let her watch him behind her without turning and scaring him off.

As much as her leg is hurting by the time she gets to the hill on the other side of Hawk Pond, she has only had to rest twice this time. She stops among the kudzu vines halfway up the hill, puts her little fingers in her mouth, and whistles, loud and sharp, the way her father taught her. She wants Coyote to associate the whistle with her, and her with food.

When she gets to the top of the hill and drops the spider stick at the side of the trail, Sadie is trotting toward her on the road. Together, Sadie frisking along-side, they head for the Davises' yard.

Coyote is where she imagined him, ears pricked toward her. There is something incredibly alert in the way he sits, as if every cell in his body is aware of her, watching her.

"Hi, Coyote!" she calls to him. He doesn't so much as twitch an ear, but he has heard her. He understands about his name, she thinks, has understood since she first thought it at him. She takes a biscuit out of her waist pack. "I brought you something!"

Before she has a chance to hold the biscuit out for Coyote to see, Sadie has jumped up and snatched it out of her hand. "No, no, no!" she yells. But Sadie has already swallowed the biscuit and is bouncing around her, yelp-ing and sniffing at the waist pack, begging for another.

Charley digs another biscuit out of the pack and throws it as far down the road as she can. Sadie dashes off to get it, and Charley turns quickly to offer the wild dog another.

He isn't there. His place by the tree is empty—just a patch of smooth, red dirt in the midst of the leaf litter and honeysuckle.

Sadie is back already, begging for another biscuit. So much for the idea of luring Coyote around the lake with biscuits, Charley thinks. She'll just have to count on his following Sadie. "Come on, dogs!" she calls. "Let's go for a walk!"

At the sound of the word, Sadie rushes ahead toward the beginning of the trail, the brush of her tail waving. Charley follows, willing Coyote to come along.

At the bottom of the hill, she looks back to see if he is following, and barely catches a glimpse of him as he scoots off the trail. She's forgotten about the mirror. When she is through the poison ivy and nearly to the spillway, she pulls out the mirror and holds it up to her left eye. Coyote, ears and tail up, is trotting down the middle of the trail.

7

One Week

It has been a week. Charley, at the dining room window, chews her lip and scratches the poison ivy rash on the inside of her elbow as she watches Coyote sneak up to the bowl of food at the end of the driveway. He still refuses to eat unless she is all the way inside the house with the door closed. A whole week she's been feeding him, and there's been no change at all. No, she thinks. There's been a change, all right. In the wrong dog.

Sadie doesn't go home anymore as soon as they get to Charley's house. Charley can't put Coyote's food out while Sadie's there, or Sadie will eat it, so she has to tie her to the railing by the side door till Coyote is finished.

The first time she tied her, Charley took Sadie a

couple of biscuits after she put Coyote's food out for him, so Sadie wouldn't feel left out. The dog books are right about patterns and routine. Sadie expects the tying now, and the biscuits. Every day when Coyote has eaten, Charley unties Sadie and Sadie hangs around for a while before she goes home. Hoping, Charley thinks, for more biscuits.

Coyote, still standing as far from the food bowl as he can, stretches his head down and snatches a few mouthfuls before backing away and checking for danger. It's almost as if he's two different creatures—the regular dog that trots along the trail or frolics with Sadie, and the wild one, the wary and terrified one Charley is watching now. He looks exactly the way he did the very first day. His tail is down, his ears back, every muscle in his body tense and ready to run.

She doesn't understand why he is so frightened. It can't be just that he's wild. Wild animals come to food. When they used to have bird feeders, the birds came right away to get the seed. And squirrels! They used to raid the feeders and wouldn't back off even if you pounded on the windows. Her mother would—

Charley stops the thought and pushes the memory away. The point is that even with a person a few feet away stomping and yelling at them, squirrels—fully wild creatures—are more interested in food than afraid of people.

For Coyote it is different. Why? What could his life have been like before he came to Eagle Lake? Without Charley's intending it, an image forms in her mind. A man is putting food at the edge of a mowed yard where the woods begin. She closes her eyes and gives herself over to the images, like watching a movie in her mind. Setting the bowl down, the man slips behind a bush a few feet away. There is a car parked on a gravel drive nearby. Another man is crouched behind the car, waiting. Coyote, nose up, materializes out of the woods. As he approaches the food, the men pounce. He is picked up and carried, struggling, to a small shed and locked inside.

Charley shivers and opens her eyes. This really happened, she thinks. She feels it the way she felt the dog's terror as he struggled to get free of the men holding him. No wonder Coyote's so wary about being fed.

All this time she's been counting on food to win him over. The books say that dogs bond readily to the person who feeds them. Feeding Coyote is supposed to show him that she's a friend, someone he can trust. But it's doing the opposite. Putting that bowl out every day only proves to him that she's dangerous, a threat. Like the Animal Control people Mrs. Davis called. No wonder the can of tuna they said would lure any dog into a trap didn't work. Coyote understands about food and humans. Food and traps.

Charley pulls a chair away from the dining room table and sits down by the window. There's nothing in the dog training books that will help her solve this problem, nothing about working with a wild and terrified dog you can't touch or even get close to, a dog you can't collar or cage or corral.

She feels like crying. She'll have to rethink her whole plan. Plan! As if she's really had one. All there was to it was the idea that walking him around the lake and feeding him every day would get him to trust her. The Taming was supposed to happen all by itself. *Food good. Charley gives food. Charley good*. Like that.

Everyone at Eagle Lake knows, now, what Charley is trying to do. Mrs. Jensen, the retired librarian who used to babysit her when she was little, is the editor of *Tail Feathers*, the newsletter that went into everybody's boxes over the weekend. She wrote a story about Charley and Coyote and asked anyone who might have been feeding him to stop so that Charley would be the only one he could go to for food.

Yesterday when Charley got around to the Davises' house, Mrs. Davis and Sadie were out on the road with

Mr. and Mrs. Sutcliff and their Labrador retriever, Boone, and Mrs. Hobbes with her little white dog, Pandy. They'd all told her what a good thing she was doing.

All the time they were standing in the road, talking, the dogs, including Coyote, had played in the Davises' yard. But when the Sutcliffs and Mrs. Hobbes went on with their walk and Mrs. Davis went inside, Coyote disappeared into the woods.

What, besides food, does she have to offer this dog? A place to live. But he has that. It isn't very comfortable—just a bare spot under a tree. If he were really wild—a fox or a coyote—he wouldn't have any more than that. A den, maybe. Coyote could probably dig himself a den if he wanted one, if he needed one.

She can offer him companionship. But he has Sadie. And the other dogs. Why would he want companionship with a human? Mrs. Hobbes told her yesterday that Coyote used to follow anyone who walked a dog around the lake, staying mostly out of sight in the woods, but still following. "It wasn't just the other dogs he was following. He wants a family. You can see it in his eyes." Charley wonders if that could be true. She thinks of the connection she felt with him the first time she saw him. It wasn't just from her to him, it was from him to her, too. He *does* want a family. He's just too afraid to know how to make it happen!

She looks out at him now, finishing the last of the food, backing away toward the woods. He needs me, she thinks. Coyotes and foxes and wolves know how to live in the wild. Dogs don't. What about winter? Every year on really cold nights, they tell people on the evening news to bring their dogs inside or make sure they have a warm, insulated shelter to go to. Coyote won't have that. He needs me. He does.

She has to come up with a way to make herself more to him than the person who puts food out for him.

"Stop that scratching!" Sarita has left her jigsaw puzzle and come into the dining room. "Don't you know the hot water trick?"

Charley hasn't realized she is scratching her arm again. "What trick?"

"Run water as hot as you can stand it on that rash until it doesn't itch anymore. That'll stop the itching all day. Eight hours, anyway. Do it again before you go to bed, and it won't itch in the night, either."

Stupid old wives' tale, Charley thinks. If that worked, why wouldn't everybody know to do it? "How do you know?"

Sarita's eyes flash. "Because I know everything!"

"Yeah, right."

"You can do it or you can go on itching. It's up to you."

Charley decides to try it. Sarita follows her into the kitchen. "So!" she says. "Not much change in that wild dog."

Charley tests the water to see how hot it is, then puts her arm under the faucet. "How long do I have to do this?"

"Like I said, till it stops itching."

"People caught him with food before," Charley says. She doesn't mention how she knows this. "Feeding scares him. I need to do something that'll give him a reason to like me. If you know everything, tell me what to do."

"What do other dogs like people for?"

Charley realizes the poison ivy really has stopped itching. She turns off the water. "Playing, I guess. Fetch. Catch. But he isn't a regular dog. He doesn't do that stuff."

"Sadie does," Sarita says.

When Charley goes out to untie Sadie, Sadie frisks around her, front paws splayed, head down, her back end in the air, tail wagging. She is begging Charley to play. Sarita's certainly right about Sadie. Charley leans down to get a dead branch that has fallen off one of the trees by the carport. As soon as she picks it up, Sadie leaps for it, trying to snatch it away. "Down!" Charley says, holding it as high in the air as she can. She throws the stick up the slope of the driveway toward where Coyote is watching from the safety of the trees. "Go get it, Sadie!"

The dog doesn't need the words. Of course not, Charley thinks, watching her tear off after the stick. Golden *retriever*.

Charley calls to Sadie to bring back the stick. She isn't as good at letting go as she is at retrieving, but Charley manages to get it away from her and throw it again. Ears flying, Sadie runs after the stick, and Charley moves up the drive, keeping an eye on Coyote, who is sitting in a tangle of honeysuckle on the other side of the road. *This is what dogs and people do together*, she thinks at him.

Sadie drops the stick and backs away from it, wagging. Charley picks it up and Sadie begins to bark, urging her to throw it. Coyote is standing now, ears and tail up, following every movement. His tail has begun to wag.

When Charley throws the stick, Sadie gets it, and Coyote comes out of the woods to join the game, chasing Sadie. After a few minutes Sadie drops the stick, and the game becomes their usual chase and grab. So focused is

Coyote that he doesn't notice when Charley moves into the middle of the yard so that the dogs have to swerve around her as they run, the way they swerve around the azaleas.

At last Sadie, tongue hanging out, flops onto the grass a few feet from where Charley is standing. Coyote circles, barking a high-pitched bark, snapping at Sadie's ears, her feet, urging her up again. When she doesn't respond, he gives up and sinks to the ground next to her. It's the closest Charley has ever been to him.

Over Sadie's shoulder, Coyote looks directly at Charley, his tongue, too, hanging out as he pants. There are big splotches of blue on his long, pink tongue. Charley has never seen anything like it.

"Blue spots on his tongue?" Sarita says later. "That's Chow. Mama or daddy or grandma maybe—that dog's got Chow in him somewhere." She is leaning over her jigsaw puzzle, squinting at a piece in her hand.

"So?" Charley says. "What does that mean?"

"It means you don't tell your father yet. Chows have a bad rep in the dog world. Blue tongue's likely to scare Paul Morgan off, end you up with some little beagle pup. Some Chihuahua."

"What's the bad rep?"

Sarita makes a little satisfied "huh" as she puts the

puzzle piece into place. "Aggressive. Protective. One-man dogs, they say. One family, anyway."

"Coyote's not aggressive. Not even with dogs. And he doesn't have a family."

Sarita shrugs and takes another piece from a cookie sheet full of bits of the sky. "Not now, anyway. You itching, by the way?"

Charley looks at the rash on her arm, surprised. "No!"

"Don't mess with me, girl!"

Charley sees a cloud piece and the place in the puzzle where it will fit, and puts it in.

"You go rest that leg," Sarita says, slapping at Charley's hand. "You been outside too long today."

Sarita is right, Charley realizes when she settles into the recliner. Her leg, her whole body, has been getting stronger this week, the walk leaving her with more energy and less pain. But after nearly two hours with the dogs, throwing a stick for Sadie sometimes, or just sitting on the fender of Sarita's car in the shade of the carport, watching them, she is worn out.

When Sadie finally swam home, her tail wagging as she went, throwing drops of water that glittered in the sun, Coyote followed her to the waterline and stood with his front feet in the water, whining. "Come back!" he seemed to be calling to her. It was as if a bungee cord stretched between the two dogs, pulling harder and harder as Sadie swam away. When she reached the other side and pulled herself out of the water next to the Davises' dock, Coyote gave one last, exasperated whine and launched himself into the water, swimming with his ears back, his tail completely underwater. The contrast between the way Sadie swam, splashing and wagging, and Coyote's grim determination made Charley laugh. This was clearly a dog who hated to swim. When he got to the other side, he dragged himself out of the water exactly where Sadie had, shook himself, and followed her up into the trees.

Charley flips the lever on the recliner and leans back, her legs stretched out in front of her. She needs to break the bungee cord that links the dogs, she thinks as she picks up the remote and turns on the television. Better yet, she needs to find a way to transfer the bungee from Sadie to herself.

8

Sadie

The next day when Charley gets to the top of the hill by Crazy Sherman's, Sadie doesn't come to her whistle. Charley doesn't see either dog, and she is all the way to the Davises' driveway before she realizes why. The SUV is gone, and Sadie is chained to a tree down near the house. Straining at the end of her chain, she barks and jumps toward Charley, her front feet pawing the air.

Coyote is lying under a rhododendron bush only a few feet from the tree Sadie is chained to. His ears are up, and he is watching Charley. Mrs. Davis has given her permission to unchain Sadie if she wants to. But Charley decides to leave Sadie chained and try to lure Coyote around the lake on his own. She throws Sadie a biscuit to make up for leaving her. "Come on," she calls to Coyote. "Let's walk!"

At the word, Coyote comes out from under the rhododendron, his tail wagging. Charley drops a biscuit on the driveway. "That's yours," she tells him, and walks away from it toward the road. With her mirror, she checks to see if he is coming to get the biscuit. He does. "Let's go get lunch!" she says, and keeps walking.

But he doesn't follow her. In the mirror she sees that he has stopped in the driveway, ears and tail down. He turns and looks back at Sadie, who is barking now and straining at the leash. Charley can almost feel the bungee cord pulling him back. The books would call this a training opportunity. She should just go on, whether he follows or not. If he doesn't come around to get his lunch today, he'll learn a lesson. He'll know to walk with her tomorrow. "Lunch!" she calls again. She puts the mirror away and starts walking again.

Every living thing is a spirit. This time Charley doesn't try to push her mother's voice out of her mind. That was what her mother believed. Charley does, too. The books are about training, controlling—human to dog. Charley wants to work with Coyote spirit to spirit. She doesn't have a book for that.

Coyote needs Sadie with him to feel safe, Charley

thinks. She understands. It's like the way she needed Amy with her on the first day of middle school. She goes back, takes Sadie off her chain, and watches the two dogs run a huge circle around the yard, bumping into each other, grabbing at each other's ears. "Let's walk!" she tells them, and they begin the walk in the way that has come to be their pattern, Sadie dashing ahead of her, Coyote following.

Near the bottom of the hill, Coyote is far behind and Sadie comes bounding back, as she always does, as if to see what is taking Charley so long. But this time she makes a lunge for Charley's walking stick and pulls it out of her hand. Charley has to grab a kudzu vine to keep from falling.

Sadie drags the stick a few feet off the trail and drops it. Then she stands by it, looking up at Charley, her tongue hanging out, her tail wagging.

"This isn't a game," Charley says. "I need that stick. Bring it back!"

Sadie gives herself a shake and trots off down the hill and across the embankment. Charley lets go of the kudzu vine and goes to get the stick, moving carefully over uneven ground through the leaf cover. Throwing sticks was a mistake yesterday. Now Sadie thinks the walking stick is a toy. She picks it up and starts back toward the trail.

Sadie comes flying back, grabs the stick, and tugs, nearly pulling Charley off her feet. Charley has to let go of it to keep from falling. Sadie trots off with the stick, carrying it back through the poison ivy, down to the edge of the pond. Then she wades out until the water is up to her chest and drops the stick into the water.

To get the stick this time, Charley will have to plough through the poison ivy, maybe wade into the pond. She looks to see where Coyote is and sees that he has stopped at the base of the hill. When she turns toward him, he watches instead of skittering off into the trees. Sadie, still standing in the water, barks. Then she splashes along the edge of the pond, bounds across the spillway, shakes herself, and starts up the hill on the other side.

Charley, furious, stands awhile longer, trying to figure out if she can get her stick back, and then gives up. She'll just have to find a replacement in the woods as she goes. When she gets to the spillway, she realizes that walking without her stick doesn't hurt much more than walking with it. At least on level ground.

Charley steps carefully, gingerly, across the spillway, balancing with her arms out on both sides as she steps from one broken chunk of concrete to the next. When she has made it to the other side, she uses the dangling root to pull herself up to the fallen tree and climbs onto it. Coyote, a few feet back on the trail, stops, waits until she's settled, then runs across the spillway and up the trail to catch up with Sadie. He passes no more than a foot from where Charley is sitting. She listens to the dogs, tussling with each other somewhere up the hill.

Coyote has always stayed behind her, ready to leap off the trail if she turns toward him. He could have gone around her, could have caught up with Sadie anytime. Has it been her walking stick keeping him back? Has he been afraid to be out ahead, where he can't keep an eye on the human with the stick? Charley laughs. It's almost as if Sadie knew that.

Charley wonders if she can manage the rest of the walk without the stick. "Till you don't need it anymore" was all Tony said when she asked how long she had to use it. Maybe, just maybe, she is done with the stick. It isn't only Coyote who'll be glad if she is. Progress. Her father will be thrilled.

9
Two Weeks

When Charley tells Mrs. Davis about how Sadie seems to have known that Coyote was afraid of her walking stick, Mrs. Davis laughs. "Don't give her too much credit, Charley. Much as we love her, she's not the brightest bulb in the pack. She's always finding sticks to play with. Your walking stick was just another toy."

Except that she didn't play with it, Charley thinks. She just took it away. What Mrs. Davis says makes sense, of course. But still—it feels as if Sadie knew what she was doing. Spirit to spirit. It's possible. Just possible.

The day Charley stopped using her stick, Sarita made a special dinner—with peach cobbler—to celebrate, and her father actually came home in time to eat it. "It's the dogs," she told them when her father said how pleased he was at her progress. "They didn't want me using the stick anymore."

"Good for them," her father said. Charley figures he doesn't believe her, but it doesn't matter. He is so glad to see her making progress, he's willing to accept anything she says.

Walking without the stick, Charley discovers that there are plenty of saplings or branches or roots to grab if she needs help over a rough bit of the trail. And without the stick, the walk with Coyote becomes very different. Sometimes he stays with Sadie, running ahead, doubling back. Though he's careful never to come close to Charley, passing her only by going through the trees off the side of the trail, it no longer seems to matter whether she is ahead of him or behind him.

Sometimes he disappears for long stretches, and she thinks they have lost him. Once in a while he vanishes almost as soon as they start the walk, and she doesn't see him again the whole way around the lake. That's when Charley worries. As many acres of woods as there are around Eagle Lake, beyond them are housing developments. Streets. Cars. And county roads where the cars go very, very fast. The images of trees, squirrels, creek that she gets when she closes her eyes don't help—she could be just imagining what she wants to believe. But always Coyote appears again by the time she and Sadie get as far as the chain across Eagle Lake Drive. It feels almost magical sometimes, the way he turns up, as if she and Sadie are wearing tracking collars that let him find them.

Little by little, he is changing. Most of the time he is his dog self now, hardly ever the wild thing. She has discovered that he can smile. It isn't just that his mouth turns up naturally—his smile, like a wagging tail, shows her how he is feeling. Even his color is changing. Some of the red in his coat turns out to have been Carolina red clay. Swimming back to Sadie's every day, his fur has gotten lighter and lighter. His tail, the ruff around his neck, and what she calls his skirts—the long hair on the backs of his legs—are a pale beige now, a real contrast to the honey gold of the rest of his coat. The toes of his front feet turn out to be white. Charley longs to pull the mats and tangles out of his tail and his skirts, to brush him and make his coat shine. She thinks he is the most beautiful dog she has ever seen. His dark chocolate eyes are lined with black all the way around, a line that slants up in the corners like the eye makeup on an Egyptian princess. "Elegant," Sarita has called him.

It is deep into the sticky North Carolina summer now, the air so thick Charley feels sometimes as if she's breathing underwater. She walks a little bit earlier every day, changing the routine gradually, in order to avoid the worst of the heat. She is still soaked with sweat by the time she gets to the Davises' house, but the walk itself is better the earlier she does it.

Now that she is sure Coyote won't run off if she doesn't bring his food to him the minute she gets home, she changes her clothes before feeding him, getting rid of the hiking boots and socks, the sweat-drenched jeans and T-shirt, putting on shorts, a tank top, and sandals. She still goes inside while he eats, and he still checks for danger every few bites, but she puts the bowl closer and closer to the house every day.

One afternoon when Sarita brings in the mail, there is a letter from Amy. Charley takes it and thinks for a moment how impressed Amy would be at the changes in Coyote, before she remembers that Amy doesn't even know about him. Incredible, she thinks, and drops the letter in the trash. She has better things to do with her time than read about how Amy is doing with her tennis.

At least she has better things to do until Sadie and Coyote swim back across the lake. After that the days have been stretching out blankly, hour after hour. She usually spends a while on the computer, answering instant messages from kids who check in to see how she's doing. Sometimes one of them asks if she wants to go to the mall or the movies, and Sarita has said she'll take her, but Charley doesn't feel like being in a car if she doesn't have to. Besides, she has discovered that she doesn't really want to leave Eagle Lake and the dogs, no matter where they are.

This time when she sits down to her laptop, Charley is thinking about the difference between working with an animal you can touch or leash or cage somehow, and a wild thing you can't control. Somebody must know how to do it. Jane Goodall. She remembers the movie they saw in science class last year about Goodall and her chimpanzees. Charley Googles Jane Goodall. An hour later she has come up with a plan. What she needs to do is spend some time in Coyote's territory.

She enlists Sarita's help, then calls Mrs. Davis to explain. Her father is working late that night, so after dinner Sarita drives Charley around the lake and drops her off in front of Crazy Sherman's.

"You can come get me when it starts to get dark."

"I'll be back before then," Sarita says.

There is a plastic bag full of freshly cooked liver chunks in Charley's waist pack. Mrs. Davis has agreed to keep Sadie inside the house every evening until dark. There's no way for this plan to work with Sadie around.

Charley whistles a couple of times to let Coyote know she's there, and walks back toward the Davises' house. Coyote is in his usual place, lying on the smooth-packed dirt by the tree across the road. "Liver!" Charley calls to him. He sits up, poised to bolt into the woods, so she stops. She takes a piece of liver out and holds it up, hoping he can smell it. "You're gonna love this."

She sets it down on the side of the road and walks away from it, back toward Sherman's. A few feet farther she puts down another piece. She keeps this up, putting a piece of liver every three feet or so, until she reaches the boulder at the end of the Heywards' driveway, one house down from the Davises'. Then she sits on the boulder, facing away from Coyote, and gets out the mirror to watch what he does. She can't see his patch of bare ground from where she is, but she can see if he comes out to get the liver.

For a long time nothing happens. She is just wondering whether she has to go even farther away when Coyote creeps out of the woods and across the road to the first piece of liver. He sniffs at it, then snatches it and gulps it down. He stands looking at the next piece, his nose quivering, and then goes just far enough to get it, walking the way he used to walk, all hunched and careful. After another moment he moves forward again and takes the next piece. And the next. Then he stops.

He knows the others are there. He can see them and smell them, and he wants them. But he won't come close enough to her to get them. Not even with her back turned. Finally he heads back across the road. He doesn't go all the way to his tree, though. He flops down under a bush, puts his nose on his paws, and watches her.

Mr. Heyward comes out to fill his bird feeder. The minute he opens the screen door, Coyote is gone into the woods. Charley explains to the man what she is doing, why she is sitting on his boulder.

"That dog's wild," he says. "If Animal Control can't catch him, nobody can."

"I don't want to *catch* him," Charley says. "I want to tame him."

"I don't know what your father's thinking of, letting you mess with that dog. That isn't some pet that got abandoned, you know. I know dogs. The way it's acting, it's never been anything *but* wild. You don't get a dog used to humans by the time it's three months old, it'll be wild forever. Wild and dangerous. That's a known fact! Can't any more tame a full-grown feral dog than you can tame a five-point buck. If it was up to me, I'd get my gun and put him down."

"You wouldn't!"

Mr. Heyward shrugs. "Come winter, it'll be the only sensible thing."

Winter's a long way away, Charley thinks. But her stomach is in a knot. Mr. Heyward goes back into his house. "Known fact," his words echo in her mind. Well, I don't know it. The books don't say anything about it. "Wild forever." No!

There *were* people in Coyote's life. What about whoever trapped him with food? Charley swats a mosquito and closes her eyes, remembering the scene she saw before, the men catching Coyote and locking him in a shed. Her breath begins to come hard and fast, the way Coyote's did, trapped in a dark shed. She sees him, *feels him* pacing back and forth, around and around, looking for a way out. He scratches at the door, at the walls, till his paws bleed. Then there is a sound by the door. Coyote smells a person coming closer and cowers back into a corner. The door opens a crack, and a child's face peers in. Coyote throws himself against the door, knocks the child down, and runs. He goes on running, into the woods.

Is this what happened? Was Coyote born in the woods? The people who owned his mother could have found him there, too late to tame him. Maybe that's who the men were who used food to catch him. And then he escaped. It could be true. Just like before, it *feels* true. She swats another mosquito and checks her mirror. Coyote has not come back.

Charley hopes he knows to stay far away from Mr. Heyward. She is just about to put the mirror back in her waist pack when he is suddenly there again, at the edge of the road. He lies down, relaxed but watchful.

Wild forever. She refuses to believe it. *You might as well get used to me*, she thinks at Coyote. *I'm not going to give up.* Come winter, she imagines a clean, brushed, golden dog curled up on the rug by the fireplace as snow falls past the bare trees outside the lake room windows. Can that happen? Of course it can. Of course.

By the time Sarita comes to get her, Charley is bored out of her mind. How did Jane Goodall keep from going nuts all those days in the jungle? She has eight new mosquito bites to add to the last of the poison ivy. She wonders if Sarita's hot water trick will work on mosquito bites. Good thing she isn't in Africa. Jane Goodall got malaria trying to get the chimpanzees used to her!

10

Rain

Coyote runs ahead of her, his blond plume of a tail waving. She follows, climbing the trail between the trees easily, both legs moving smoothly, fast. She is not carrying a spider stick because there are no spiders. Just the clean, clear, bright air. Not like summer. Like the perfect days of spring. Or fall, maybe. Except that the leaves haven't turned color. When she reaches the top of the hill, she breaks into a run, amazed at the freedom of it, dodging low-hanging branches and weaving in and out between trees and stands of Russian olive, until she and Coyote are side by side, emerging together into the sunlight. They are on a huge granite boulder overlooking the lake, the glitter of the water, the sweep of sky stretching before them. Charley sits on the edge, her legs dangling over toward the water below, and Coyote sits a little *way away, too far to touch, but closer than he's ever been. He turns to look at her, his eyes intent on her face, his ears pointed sharply forward. The sun makes diamonds on the lake as a breeze ruffles the water.* Listen. *Her heart leaps. It is her mother's voice, coming from directly behind her.* Listen! *Charley turns to see her mother. There is nothing there but the rough granite of the boulder, the pale green circles of lichen.*

Charley opens her eyes to dull gray light. Rain pounds steadily on the roof. She holds the sheet tight against her chin, wishing she could go back to the dream, back to the moment she heard her mother's voice, clear and real and not a memory, the moment she believed her mother had come back, was really there. No good. Even if she could get that moment back, there would, inevitably, be the next, when she turned and saw the empty stretch of granite. Stupid to have been tricked into believing, even in a dream. There is no clearing in the woods above the lake, no boulder like the one she and Coyote were sitting on. And no way for her mother to come back.

The clock says 8:32. She has slept later than she has in weeks. There is no sun to filter through the blinds and wake her. Coyote will be wondering where she is.

Charley has never thought about having to walk the

trail in the rain. The drought has gone on so long, she's almost forgotten the possibility of rain. Already she's late. She should be at the Davises' by now, starting back. She gets out of bed, goes to the window, looks out between the slats of the blind. It is like peering into a deep green jungle through a curtain of silvery beads. What she can see of the sky is leaden, no cloud forms moving, no scraps of blue giving hope for clearing.

It is Day Nineteen of The Taming—Saturday, Sarita's day off. She can hear her father in the kitchen, banging things. It's the way he always is in the kitchen, slamming cupboard doors, clanging silverware, smacking bowls or plates on the counter, as if he's mad at them. He can make the opening of a box of cereal sound like small arms fire.

This isn't what he used to be like, when he and her mother sometimes worked together to make wonderful, special dinners. He always did the meat dish, her mother the vegetables and salad. What he wants now, Charley thinks, is for someone else to be doing all of it, whatever has to be done. He hates cooking now, hates having to think about food except to eat it. Hates having to clean up afterward.

If he could have hired Sarita twenty-four/seven, he would have, so that he would never, ever have to set foot in the kitchen. Before the accident Charley used to shoo him out on Sarita's day off sometimes and do it herself, even the cleanup. Breakfast and lunch were easy—cereal, sandwiches, whatever. And there was enough stuff she'd learned to make—tuna casserole, macaroni and cheese, hot dogs and beans—to get them through dinner once or even twice a week.

Since March he's had to do Saturdays himself. Charley could take over in the kitchen again now, and she knows it. He knows it, too, and the banging is getting louder. But he hasn't ordered Charley to do it, or even asked her. Until he does, she isn't going to volunteer.

She writes the number 19 on the calendar and dresses for the walk. She can't expect Coyote not to eat just because it's raining. As she laces her hiking boots, she wonders what the dog is doing in the rain, where he has gone for shelter. His place under the sweet gum isn't really a den. The leaves overhead are the only protection. From the sound of the rain on the roof, that won't be worth much today. The image of him huddled, nose to tail, rises in her mind. His ears are tipped sideways, and he's lying beneath something that doesn't provide the cover he needs. She watches a thin stream of water fall onto his forehead, run down his nose.

"You going out?" Dad asks when she gets to the

kitchen. He is leaning against the counter, eating a piece of toast.

Charley nods and gets out a bowl for cereal. "Coyote needs to eat."

"Seems to me if he's all that hungry, he should be coming around to get his food on his own by now. It's been—what?—three weeks?"

"Nineteen days."

Her father pours himself a second cup of coffee and bangs the empty pot back into the coffeemaker. "You sure this is going to work?"

"I'm sure." She isn't, not really.

"You shouldn't walk that trail when the weather's like this."

"It's only rain," Charley says. As she says the words, they become a kind of echo. *It's only rain.* Her mother used to say that whenever she set off for the woods with her cameras under her yellow slicker. Her mother loved the way the world looked on a day like this. Eventually there was a whole series of photos—soft colors, misty air, silvery drops on the tips of leaves. *Rainy Day Carolina.* The series won an award somewhere.

Charley concentrates on pouring cereal into her bowl, getting out the milk, pouring it, putting it back into the refrigerator. Cereal. Milk. Eating. Breathing in and out, chewing, swallowing. Stay focused, she reminds herself firmly. No remembering.

"How long will you be?" Paul Morgan asks, his voice carefully light, as if he has no particular interest in the answer.

"About an hour. Why?"

"Mrs. Jensen's gone to the mountains. She can't come stay with you, and I need to go to the office."

Of course he does. "You can go."

"Not while you're out there in the woods by yourself. You could slip and fall. You could—"

"Hurt myself?" she finishes for him. "I hurt all the time." Even without looking, she can feel him wince. She probably ought to be sorry, but she isn't. Why shouldn't he feel bad about running away to his office on Saturday, for never, never being there? "You don't have to worry about me. I'll be fine."

Her father looks out the window and sips his coffee. "I'll stay here till you get back. I just need to go in for a few hours. I'll stop on the way home and get takeout for dinner."

Charley grins into her cereal bowl. These days her father even manages to bang Styrofoam boxes.

She considers, briefly, taking an umbrella. But if Coyote doesn't like walking sticks, she's pretty sure an umbrella would freak him out. She wears her slicker instead. Before she gets as far as Mr. Garrison's, where Jasmine and Bernie are holed up in their twin doghouses, not even barking as she passes, she is sweating under the slicker. She takes down the hood and lets the cool rain fall on her hair and face.

The world really is different on a day like this, she thinks. There is a new smell, almost a taste to the air. The colors are softened, the edges of things blurred. Only sound is sharper—the family of five geese honking from the water could be right there on the trail with her. Mrs. Jensen says the geese are the pair that raised three goslings on the lake last year, back again with their whole family. No one can know this for sure, Charley thinks. How could it be that wild things born here can fly away to another part of the world and come back again, not having been shot by hunters, caught by foxes, hit by lightning?

When Charley gets to the road and whistles, Sadie doesn't come running. Coyote isn't under his tree. She sees that neither of the Davises' cars is in the driveway and Sadie is chained on the side deck. She is lying up under the eaves, out of the wet.

"Where's Coyote?" Charley calls. Sadie comes to the end of the chain and barks, her tail wagging eagerly. She seems to have no problem with the prospect of a walk in the rain.

As Charley starts down the driveway, Coyote crawls out from beneath the picnic table in the side yard. He is drenched, his fur darkened and muddy. The picnic table, its boards spaced half an inch apart, has offered little shelter from the rain overhead and none at all from the water running down the yard toward the lake. He shakes himself, spraying mud and water, and then waits at the edge of the woods for Sadie to be released.

It's only rain, Charley tells herself. But Coyote looks awful. Miserable.

"Shelter," she calls to him. "I'm offering you food *and* shelter. Remember that!"

He wants both, she thinks. From the tilt of his ears, it is clear that he doesn't like rain any more than he likes swimming.

Once they start the walk, though, Coyote and Sadie pay no attention to the rain. They bound off on one side of the trail, then the other, doubling back and charging ahead, bumping into each other from time to time the way they do when they're playing. After a while Coyote disappears on some journey of his own. Charley listens, hoping to be able to hear where he has gone. There is something about this day that makes her want him with her. Close. Safe. But there is no holding him.

She has passed the worst of the steep, slippery part of the trail, moving from handhold to handhold, has ducked under the Limbo Tree, and is heading across the ridge of the hill when she catches her foot in a vine and falls, landing full length in a thick patch of poison ivy with such force that the breath is knocked out of her. For a moment everything seems to stop except the pain in her leg and the steady fall of the rain. *It's only rain.*

When she is able to breathe again, Charley discovers, with a jolt of surprise, that she is crying. Tears are sliding down her cheeks, the only difference between rain and tears the warmth of the tears. Sadie comes back along the trail and nudges her with her nose.

"Leave me alone," Charley says. She tries to blink back the tears, but they are flowing faster now. She doesn't know why she is crying, but she needs to make it stop. She folds her arms beneath her head and puts her forehead on the wetness of her slicker, its yellow bright against the deep green of the ivy leaves. She squeezes her eyes as tightly shut as she can, willing the tears away. Stop it. Now. She swallows hard, and little by little the tears begin to slow. When at last the wetness on her face is just the rain, she lies very still, breathing and counting, breathing and counting. She feels Sadie's nose against her neck and turns her head to tell her to go away.

It isn't Sadie. For the space of a single breath, Coyote's nose is an inch from hers. His dark eyes meet hers.

Listen. Listen.

Charley reaches a hand toward Coyote, and he backs hurriedly away. Still there is no taking back what has just happened. He has touched her. Dog to human. Spirit to spirit. She can still feel his nose on her neck. She pushes her hair out of her eyes with a muddy hand. *Listen!* It is what her mother used to say when she sat, camera in her hands, Charley on the ground nearby, waiting for the right light, the perfect puff of wind, a bird or squirrel or lizard to venture into view.

Charley listens now, the way she used to when her mother told her to. She can hear the rain on the leaves over her head, on the ground around her. She hears a stir of wind, a bird calling across the lake, Sadie moving in the soggy leaf litter down the hill. She doesn't know now any more than she knew then what it is she is listening for, what her mother wanted her to hear.

She sits up, rubs her hands on her wet jeans, and then,

with the help of a hickory sapling, drags herself to her feet. Coyote is ahead of her on the trail, moving slowly, his bedraggled tail waving in the rain. "Coyote!" she calls.

He glances over his shoulder and goes on.

"Thank you," she says. "Thank you."

11

Trees and Stones . . .

The Morgan house, like most of the houses on Eagle Lake, was built into the hillside above the lake. The upper floor was originally all there was, the lower floor having been added on the lake side later by remodeling the garage and building an addition. It is on the lower floor that Sarita lives, in what used to be the garage—a big room with a sink, a tiny refrigerator, and a couch that opens into a bed. Beyond Sarita's room, past the stairs that come down from the lake room above, past a hallway with a bathroom, behind a perpetually closed door, is the addition—Charley's mother's studio.

Charley stands in the shadowy dark hallway, staring at the closed door. It *was* her mother's studio, she thinks. What it is now is something else again. Storeroom.

Warehouse. Museum. She has not gone into it, the way she hadn't walked the woods trail, since she was ten years old and her mother's real voice, her real, living, breathing self, filled it with activity and life.

Sadie and Coyote have gone. As soon as Coyote finished eating, they swam the lake in the rain and disappeared beneath the Davises' trees. Still wearing her slicker, she stood on the dock and watched them go. Her father left moments later, and Charley was alone with the rain. The empty day, in the empty house, stretched ahead of her like a trek across the wilderness. If the rain continued, she wouldn't even go to sit on the boulder and play Jane Goodall in Coyote's territory.

She took a shower, scrubbing carefully to get rid of the poison ivy oil, washed and dried her hair, put on clean clothes, and considered fixing herself something to eat. She tried to find a movie she wanted to watch on television. She picked up and put down three books, and then she crept down the stairs, feeling like an intruder as she moved through Sarita's room and into the hall.

Her mother's voice has been in her head since she fell on the trail—*listen, listen.* Since before that. Since the dream. It is what brought her here, as if she is following the sound. Now she watches her hand reach for the knob, the way a camera would focus close in a movie, and opens the door. She stands at the open door, listening to the rain pound on the roof over her head, and then steps inside.

Dust. Silence. She touches the wall switch, and the long room is flooded with light. Too much light. Quickly she turns it off and goes to the desk by the nearest window to turn on a reading lamp. Her mother's photographs, some framed, some only matted, cover almost every inch of wall above the built-in cabinets that line much of the room. Each one is a photo of some bit of Eagle Lake. Her mother believed that all of nature could be found in any part of it. "I don't have to go any farther than our woods," she used to say.

Until someone who had seen her work lured her away to a rainforest in Brazil. Charley would never know why her mother went, what she found there. Whatever pictures she took vanished from the world as completely as she did when the plane went down.

On the floor, leaning against one leg of the worktable that takes up the center of the room, their brown paper-covered backs facing her, are the framed photos Charley took down from the walls of her room the day of the funeral. She doesn't even remember now what they are. She leans down to turn the first one around. Mistake. Seeing it is like a blow to the stomach. It is the picture her mother took for her of the fairy castle.

It isn't really a fairy castle, of course. It is only the stump of an ancient pine tree, broken off a foot or so above the ground. The black-and-white photo was taken early one morning, when mist was still rising from the moss in the first rays of morning sun. The plates of the pine tree's bark, layer after thin layer, form a jagged ring of concentric circles—the castle's battlements—around the central core, a space like a courtyard, carpeted with moss. In the middle of the courtyard a tower of splintered wood, crusted with lichen, rises another foot. Between two roots a hole leads into darkness beneath— like an entrance to the mysterious interior.

It was Charley who named it the fairy castle, playing there while her mother took photographs or waited to take them. A million times she must have imagined herself going into the hole between the roots, down into darkness and then up again into the candlelit, glittery rooms of the castle. The kitchen, the bedrooms, the dining hall.

The stump must still be out there, just a plain old stump like plenty of others, probably nearly hidden now by leaves that have never been brushed away, as she used to do to keep the courtyard clear, the entrance open. But it was magical when she was little enough to believe—

almost believe—in fairies. The photograph used to hang on the wall across from her bed, where she could see it as soon as she opened her eyes. Even now she can almost see a figure standing in the castle courtyard dressed in shades of brown and green, slim and winged like a dragonfly with transparent, iridescent double wings.

Charley turns the photo around again and straightens up. The cheerful, friendly clutter that was her mother's way of working has been tidied away. Her father—or Sarita—has packed most of her mother's belongings into boxes that stand open on the table. By the door at the far end of the room that leads outside, boxes are stacked on the daybed under the window. The bigger equipment has been draped with cloth, standing now like hulking ghosts. The door to the darkroom stands ajar, the sign that used to warn Charley away when the darkroom was in use hanging crooked from its hook. She has been right to stay away from here, she thinks.

She goes to turn off the lamp and notices a stack of books on the desk. They are new and all the same—a coffee table book she has never seen before. *Trees and Stones Will Teach You* by Colleen Morgan. Charley stares at her mother's name. Colleen Morgan. What use is a name when there is no person to attach it to, no person to answer if you say it aloud? The book's cover photo, taken from the water, is of the sweet gum her mother called Tree.

Surrounded by woods, thousands and thousands of trees, her mother loved this one best. Somewhere in these cabinets, in these drawers, Charley thinks, there must be hundreds of photos of Tree. In every season, in every kind of weather, in every kind of light.

"Weed trees," people call sweet gums. When a pair of beavers started chewing the bark of Eagle Lake trees, the community considered getting someone in to kill the beavers and save the woods, until they found out that beavers have a preference for sweet gums. "They can take all of those they want!" the president of the board said. Charley's mother pointed out later that the beavers never laid a tooth on Tree.

"He's a survivor," she said. Enormously tall, Tree was growing on the hillside above the creek more than seventy years ago when the dam was built. As the water rose, the lake gradually surrounded Tree so that it was growing almost completely in the water. Other trees along the waterline gradually died, their roots drowned, but Tree stayed on, green, then red, then bare boned, then green again. Charley went with her mother to see Tree by water more times than she could remember. Her mother would pull the canoe against his trunk, touch him, talk to him.

Charley picks up the book on top of the stack, opens it, and leafs through the pages. Like most of the books her mother took photographs for, this one has more pictures than words. Across from each photo is a short poem or a quotation. On the title page is the rest of the title quotation: "'Trees and stones will teach you that which you can never learn from masters.' — St. Bernard of Clairvaux."

Charley looks at the cover photo again. Tree stands out against the green shrubs of the hillside, his trunk centered between the deep red of his autumn leaves above and their reflection in the water from which he grows. Survivor. How can a tree live in water more than seventy years and the human who loved and admired him vanish in an instant half a world away from home?

Charley turns out the light and leaves the studio, carefully closing the door behind her. She shouldn't have come, she thinks. But she takes the book with her.

12

Photographs

Charley takes the book to her room and drops it on her bed. Then she stands, listening to the rain, aware of the emptiness around her, thinking about going back to her chair in the lake room, finding a funny movie to watch on television—a movie that will take her away from Eagle Lake, make her laugh. But she doesn't go. The book, its doubled image of Tree in autumn, holds her like a magnet. Colleen Morgan, award-winning nature photographer. Where is she now? How can it be that her mother just *isn't* anymore?

Finally she settles onto the bed, fluffs her pillow behind her, switches on her reading light, and begins to turn the pages slowly, looking at the photographs, reading the quotations. Colleen Morgan might be gone, but her work, the last work she finished, is here.

As often as Charley went into the woods with her mother while she was working, the pictures she took there were always a surprise. It was as though the camera saw a different world than Charley did. Small things got bigger. Or big things got smaller. Edges blurred in the mist, colors sharpened in the slant of late afternoon sun, shadows deepened, the sun sparked individual diamonds and streaks of brilliant light on the surface of the water where there had been only ripple and glitter.

The stillness of the picture caught a moment that would have been different for Charley even if she had been sitting exactly where the camera was at exactly the same moment, looking at exactly the same thing. For her the bird would have moved its head, the leaf would have shifted in the wind, the spider would have walked along the strand of its web. She never understood how her mother could know what the camera would hold in place, how she even saw the image she wanted to catch. One of the photos in the book shows a cedar waxwing on a bare winter branch, leaning to place a dogwood berry into the beak of another cedar waxwing. How had she caught that moment? How had she even known to have her camera ready?

It is a question Charley never thought to ask when

her mother was there. She was too young to wonder then, too young to care about the work her mother did. She had expected her mother to be there, in her world, in her life, as long as she needed her.

Now, this minute, Charley wants more than anything to ask her mother this question. How did she do what she did? That isn't all she wants to know. She wants to know why. Why photography? Why nature?

And why did she change her mind and go off to take pictures of the rainforest?

Charley looks at the copyright date in the book. It came out after her mother was gone. This is the book Colleen Morgan was talking about, working on, finding quotations and choosing photos for, just before she left for Brazil. She never saw the finished book. Would she have been satisfied with it? Would she have liked it?

Charley wonders which she chose first, the photos or the words. On the page across from the cedar waxwings Charley reads, "'Love cannot be forced, love cannot be coaxed and teased. It comes out of Heaven, unasked and unsought.'—Pearl Buck."

She turns the page. The next photo was taken in the Morgans' yard, easy to recognize because theirs is one of only three houses on the lake that has a lawn. Everyone else has just the woods, shrubs, with a garden here or there in whatever sunlight can be had among the trees. The photo is a tight close-up, the blades of grass huge, like a dense green forest, bright above, shadowy at the base. A ladybug on one blade, shiny in the sunlight, is the size of a dime. Across from that page are the words "'Every blade of grass has its Angel that bends over it and whispers, "Grow, grow."'—The Talmud."

There are no angels. Only grass and ladybug.

Charley remembers her mother mowing the grass. The images are hazy—raggedy blue jeans, green-stained sneakers. No face. Like the way, sometimes, in a dream, she knows who someone is but can't quite see them.

Colleen Morgan hated having a whole yard full of grass that needed cutting, hated cutting it, but it was a job she never let her husband do. She would pull the cord to start the mower, and then shout for all the living things hiding in the grass to get out of the way. She would move very slowly, stopping if she saw a cricket or a katydid that wasn't moving out of the way fast enough. "Head for the *short* grass!" she'd yell. "I won't be coming back over what I've already cut." If she saw a toad in front of her, she would stop the mower altogether and move the toad out of the way, dropping it among the azalea bushes or in the flower garden at the front of the house.

Charley remembers a summer when her mother found a yellow jacket nest in the grass by the willow tree she'd planted as part of her campaign to replace lawn with trees. Mr. Sutcliff was always being stung by the yellow jackets in his yard. "The first one that stings you puts a smell on you," he told Charley once, "and the rest come after you then. Get stung one time, you'll get stung fifty times." Charley and her mother saw him one day when they were out in the canoe, running from his mower, waving his arms around his head. He dashed into his house, yelling and flailing, and slammed the door. For days afterward his mower sat abandoned as the grass grew taller around it. "If you get yellow jackets, you have to go out in the middle of the night and pour gasoline or boiling water down their hole," he told them.

But her mother didn't do that. The first day she found the nest, she stood near it as yellow jackets came and went, talking to them. "I've got to mow," she told them, "but I don't want to hurt you. You can just keep coming and going until I tell you that the next pass will go over the nest. Then you have to either go down inside or stay out till I've passed over. It'll just take a minute or two, and then you can go back to business as usual."

Her father teased her about it all summer—"My wife, the wasp whisperer." But Colleen Morgan never got stung a single time. Charley asked her why she didn't tell Mr. Sutcliff that he didn't have to use gasoline, but she said it was better not to challenge people's fixed beliefs. The next year the wasps didn't nest in the Morgans' yard.

Her father does the mowing now, and he just mows, not worrying about what might be in his way. But they've never had yellow jackets again. Mr. Sutcliff still gets stung every summer.

Charley touches the photo, feeling the slick surface under her fingers, as if by touching this page she could touch her mother as she lay in the grass, focusing her lens on a ladybug walking a green blade.

She flips through pages then, skimming, not really looking, not reading, till a photo stops her. It is a beaver, crouched in the water at the edge of the lake among some sort of leafy plants, its wet fur slicked back, silver water drops scattered along its back. It holds a piece of green plant in its front paws, its eyes staring straight off into the distance as if it has stopped eating to consider something.

It is not a picture her mother could have taken when Charley was with her. As hard as she tried, she was never quiet enough for that. If a beaver heard the slightest sound, a twig breaking, a sigh or a cough or a sniffle, it would be gone with a resounding crack of tail against water. Charley doesn't know how her mother stayed quiet enough. She never made a blind for herself, never hid from the animals she photographed. She just sat still and waited.

"'To understand any living thing,'" the quotation on the facing page says, "'you must creep within and feel the beating of its heart.'—W. Macneille Dixon."

Creep within and feel the beating of its heart. Yes. That's what Charley wants to do with Coyote.

The rain is still drumming on the roof, and she thinks of Coyote huddled under the Davises' picnic table, taking what shelter he can from the rain. The Davises are probably home by now, probably have Sadie inside where she can be drying off. There is nowhere for Coyote to go to get dry. What is he feeling? What is he thinking? Do dogs think?

She closes the book. *Creep within and feel the beating of its heart.* Impossible. She can't even feel her own.

13

Miracle

It is early afternoon. Charley has eaten her lunch at the table on the gravel terrace down by the lake, where it is shady. While she ate, Sadie lay at her feet, hoping for a piece of sandwich. Coyote stayed under the camellia bush next to the terrace, as close to Sadie as he could get without getting too close to Charley. She has saved some crusts from her sandwich and now that she is finished, gives one to Sadie and throws the other to Coyote. He jumps up and backs away, as if it is a stone she's thrown, but when Sadie starts over to get his crust, he snatches it before she can get near.

Charley hears Bethanne Davis calling for Sadie from across the lake. Sadie's ears prick up, but she keeps her eyes on Charley in case there are any more treats. "Sorry, girl," Charley says. "That's all there is. Guess you'll just have to go home."

Bethanne calls again, and then Mrs. Davis whistles, and Sadie heads down to the water. She stands for a moment before starting across, her big, gold plume of a tail waving gently as she tries to decide whether to stay or go. When Bethanne calls once more, she jumps forward into the water and starts swimming.

Coyote follows her to the lake, as always, and stands with his front feet in the water, watching Sadie swim. When she is about halfway across, he whines, but doesn't start after her. She gets all the way across, climbs out of the water, shakes herself, and runs up the hill. Still Coyote doesn't move. He will go any minute, Charley thinks. Of course he will. Much as he hates swimming, he always follows Sadie eventually.

But he doesn't. He stands awhile longer, looking toward where she has disappeared, and then turns around, goes back to the camellia bush, and lies down. Sadie has gone home and Coyote has stayed. He's made a choice. Between Charley and Sadie, he's chosen Charley.

At first she doesn't move. She is afraid if she does anything, makes even the slightest sound, he will realize what he's done and take off.

Liver. She needs to get him some liver, reward him for staying. Slowly, carefully, looking away from him every minute, she eases herself out of the chair and starts up to the house. "Good dog!" she says as she goes, her voice as low and soothing as she can make it. "Just stay there. Good old boy!"

"Sarita!" she yells when she gets inside. "You'll never..." But Sarita must have been watching from the windows by her puzzle table. She is already coming from the kitchen with the sandwich bag full of liver pieces.

Coyote is still under the camellia. Charley wants to run down the drive and throw herself at him, hug him and rub his ears as if he's a regular dog. *Her* regular dog! It is all she can do to walk slowly down to the terrace, keeping her eyes focused on the table and chairs, and sit down. "Good dog!" she says again, amazed and relieved that he is still there. "Want some liver?"

She has been talking to him about the liver she takes him every evening, saying the word over and over as he comes to get the pieces she puts out so that he'll know that the word means something he really, really likes. And he's been coming gradually closer and closer to get it. But still he hasn't taken the pieces closest to her. She always sees him as she and Sarita drive away, sneaking back to get the last of them.

She turns to look at him now, and their eyes meet. He doesn't bolt. She feels the tremor of their connection. "Liver!" she says. "Every time you stay here when Sadie goes home, you get to have liver!" She takes the biggest piece she can find, holds it between her thumb and first finger so that it sticks out away from her hand, turns her head away, and holds the liver out to him as far as her arm will reach.

Is he coming to get it? She can't tell. She doesn't dare turn to see. She holds her breath, makes herself as still as she can. *Come on*, she thinks at him, *you can do it. Come get the liver!*

And suddenly the liver is gone from her fingers. He has taken it so gently she didn't feel his muzzle near her hand. Just one moment the liver between her fingers and the next moment gone. Moving in slow motion, she pulls her hand back and gets another piece of liver. She extends her arm again, and again the liver disappears. Three more times she does it. Then she holds the last piece out in her cupped palm so that he'll have to touch her to get it. It takes longer this time, but he gets it, his nose and whiskers grazing her hand.

At his touch her eyes blur with tears. "Good dog," she whispers. "Good, brave dog!" The sandwich bag is empty now, so she turns to look at him. He is no more than two feet away. He stands his ground, his ears and tail up, look-ing at her as if to ask if there is any more.

"All gone," she says, and shows him her empty hands. He stands for another moment, and then turns and goes back to the camellia. He doesn't run, he doesn't skulk. He just walks back and lies down.

Charley looks up at the windows of the lake room above her. Sarita is there, watching. She smiles and nods, and Charley holds up both thumbs. "Wild forever," Mr. Heyward said. Not this dog!

Coyote stays in the yard the rest of the day. When Charley's father comes home, he scuttles across the road into the woods for a little, but comes back to his place under the dogwood when Paul Morgan goes inside.

Charley calls Mrs. Davis and tells her that Coyote stayed when Sadie went home. "That's fabulous, Charley," she says. "The kids said they hadn't seen him, and I was a little worried. I thought something might have happened to him."

"He's fine."

"Looks like your hard work is paying off."

"Anyway, if he stays over here you won't have to keep Sadie inside tonight."

Mrs. Davis laughs. "And you won't have to risk

hearing Buddy Heyward tell you how impossible and dangerous this whole project is!"

After dinner Charley's father goes back to the office. At the time she would normally have gone around to Coyote's territory with the liver, Charley splashes on insect repellent again and goes out to sit on the brick retaining wall. Coyote, under the dogwood, stays where he is, his eyes on her. "Brought your liver," she says. His ears flick toward her. She holds a piece out toward him, but he doesn't move. "Suit yourself," she says.

Half an hour later she goes inside, leaving three pieces of liver on the wall where she was sitting. Before she gets to the top of the ramp, he has snatched and gulped them down. Then he goes back to settle into his place again.

The lights on the ramp are on a timer, set to go on before it gets completely dark. A little while after they come on, Charley goes out to check on Coyote. He isn't by the fence where he was before. She checks under the camellia, behind the boxwoods, even goes out to look among the azaleas. He is not there.

When she goes back inside, Sarita looks up from her jigsaw puzzle, a painting of the Cape Hatteras lighthouse. The television is on. Other people *watch* television, Charley thinks. Sarita only listens while she does her puzzles.

"He's gone," Charley says. She had hoped he would stay the night.

Sarita nods. "A good day, though," she says, and fits a piece into the stream of light cutting across a bank of storm clouds.

The moment she says it, Charley knows that it's more than good. It's the best day she's had all summer.

14

Watchdog

When Charley goes out the next morning, dressed to walk around the lake as always, Coyote appears from the trees across the road and stands at the head of the driveway, looking at her.

She can hardly believe her eyes. "Good morning, Coyote!" she calls, then spreads out both of her arms like a mother inviting a child to come running for a hug. He doesn't come. But he doesn't back off, either. His tail, a pale golden plume, stands straight up over his back, and she thinks she sees it move, the beginning of a wag. "Want your lunch?" she asks, thinking it is time to change the word to *breakfast* if he is going to eat it first thing in the morning like this.

But he does know the word. As soon as she says it, he

takes a few hesitant steps down the drive. Then he sits, watching her expectantly.

"Okay. I'll be right out with it!"

When she takes his bowl outside, he scuttles off into the trees. She puts it down where she has been feeding him lately, on the driveway near his place by the dogwood. Then she goes to sit on the retaining wall. "Come and get it!" she calls.

He emerges from the woods onto the road. His tail is down, now, and his ears back, his shoulders hunched forward. He is a wild thing again.

"What's the matter?" Charley asks. "You took liver from my hand last night!"

At the word *liver* his ears twitch, but he doesn't relax. He's been eating with her sitting and watching for days. What is the problem?

And then she knows. The problem is that Sadie isn't here. It's just him and Charley. "It's okay," she tells him. "Really it is! You took liver from my hand yesterday, remember? Sadie wasn't with you then."

But that was yesterday. There was a night to get through since then. Wherever he was, like all his other nights, he was alone. Alone meant having to be on guard, watch out, survive, even while he slept.

Besides, sleeping can wipe out memory so that you

have to start over again in the morning. Charley knows how it is to wake up in your old self and all over again have to get used to what has changed in your life.

"Okay, guy," she says. She goes back into the house. Almost the instant the door slides shut, Coyote comes down the drive and eats. He still leans forward and snatches no more than a bite or two between glances over his shoulder. But he eats, and when he is finished, he flops down in his place under the dogwood.

Later, when Charley is reading on the terrace, a fishing boat comes by, its electric trolling motor making a barely perceptible hum. Coyote goes down to the bushes at the edge of the lake and barks at it. "That's some new watchdog you've got there," Mr. Sutcliff shouts over the barking.

Coyote barks until the boat has gone on down the lake and even the ripples have faded. Then he comes back to lie down under the camellia. Charley imagines him congratulating himself for having chased off a dangerous enemy. This barking is another step forward, she thinks. Their yard has become Coyote's territory.

That day a new pattern begins. The daily hikes are over. After dinner Charley takes Coyote his liver pieces, and little by little he begins to come up to her and take them from her hand, even when she's looking at him. At dusk he disappears. But when she goes outside in the morning, he is there, lying up by the road or sitting at the end of the driveway, waiting for her. If her father leaves before Charley goes out, he never sees the dog, but Charley is sure Coyote isn't going back around the lake anymore. He has found a place in the woods across the road to spend the night.

Sadie comes over later, sometimes swimming, sometimes on the road. Charley always has a book with her, but she doesn't get much reading done. After a while she figures out what the dogs are telling each other with their ears and their tails and the expressions on their faces. If she kept a notebook like Jane Goodall did with the chimpanzees, she thinks, it would have more interesting information about dogs than the training books do.

The only change in the new pattern happens on the Fourth of July. Fireworks aren't legal in North Carolina, but they are in South Carolina, and Eagle Lake is only a few miles from the South Carolina border, so there are plenty of firecrackers and bottle rockets around the lake on the Fourth. The minute the firecrackers start going off in the early afternoon, Coyote disappears. Charley and her father and Sarita have been invited to the Sutcliffs' for a picnic supper, along with most of the rest of the people from the north side of the lake. Coyote hasn't shown up again when it's time for them to leave, so he doesn't get his evening liver. She leaves a few pieces on the retaining wall.

When they get home after the picnic, there is no sign of Coyote. The liver is still on the wall. Deep booms fill the night from the official fireworks in downtown Charlotte. Charley worries all night about where Coyote is and whether he'll come back. She's heard of dogs so frightened by fireworks that they run off and get lost and are never seen again. But when she goes out the next morning, the liver is gone and he is there, lying out by the road.

Just taking care of myself, he seems to say. You can't be too careful.

15

Five Weeks

> "'When we try to pick out anything by itself, we find it hitched to everything else in the universe.' —John Muir."

_____

*C*harley is sitting on her bed, looking at her mother's book. The photo that goes with this quotation is a perfect circle of white mushrooms, some big, some small, against a background of brilliant green moss. A fairy ring. The mushrooms, she knows, are attached to one another—are really only a single fungus, its connections underground. It is called a fairy ring because it seems to appear by magic, overnight. One day it isn't there; the next it is. In a few days it will be gone, as if the fairies came to dance there in the moonlight and then moved on, leaving their magic to fade.

Charley remembers believing that. She remembers being in this place when a fairy ring was there, begging to be allowed to stay out at night to watch. "If humans are there, the fairies won't come," her mother told her.

Later, of course, she gave up the idea of fairies dancing in the moonlight. But this place where the photo was taken remained a special place, different from the rest of the Eagle Lake woods of beech and hickory, oak and sweet gum, dogwood and sourwood. Her mother called it the Pine Grove—a small hillock covered entirely with evergreens—pines and cedars and holly. Charley doesn't remember exactly where it is, but she knows it isn't on the lake trail. In all the days of walking around the lake, she hasn't passed it.

Sitting with the book open on her lap, staring at the fairy ring, Charley has a strange sensation. It's as if she is looking through her mother's eyes. She can almost feel the camera in her hands, the pine needles and small stones under her as she kneels to get exactly this angle, this contrast of green and white, shadows of pine boughs on the moss.

Goose bumps rise along her arms. She reaches to close the book and finds her mother's face looking at her from a photo on the back jacket flap. Colleen Morgan, dark hair, blue eyes, splotches of pink on her cheeks against skin as pale as skim milk. Her mother called those splotches her "continents"—the shape of South America on one cheek, Africa on the other—proof of the Irish heritage that Charley shares. Charley touches her own cheek now, feeling the surge of heat, knowing that if she had a mirror she would see the pink that for her appears only when feelings rise like a tidal wave and threaten to wash her away. It doesn't matter what the feelings are— anger, embarrassment, this rush of loss—her cheeks broadcast it to the world.

She did not know there was a picture of her mother in this book. It has been hiding like a scorpion, waiting to sting. She pushes the book back under her pillow, pulls the sheet up over it, piles the other pillow on top. Her throat has closed so that she almost cannot swallow at all.

The woods, Charley thinks. What she wants at this moment is to get out into the woods, away from the book, the house, the human world.

She hasn't walked the trail since Coyote began spending the night on this side of the lake. She realizes now how much she has missed the woods. How much she has missed the sounds of the birds, the pattern of sunlight through the leaves, the rustle of wind in the trees. She even misses spider sticks, and the way the silvery threads they catch glint in the sun.

Two whole years. How could she have stayed away from the woods she grew up in, the woods that had been the background, the setting, for her whole life? Two years ago she made herself a new life, with a new setting, just the way her father did. His life became work, hers became school, Amy and her brother, and their friends. Two summers at Amy's house, swimming in their pool—a pool surrounded by concrete and grass and a tall wooden fence—two summers of malls and movies.

Coyote must be missing the woods, too, she thinks. For the dogs the walk through the woods is never just a way to get from one place to another. It is always an adventure.

She changes into her hiking clothes, calls to Sarita to tell her she's going out. Coyote is under the dogwood. "Walk!" Charley says to him. "Let's go for a walk." He gets up and stretches, first his front legs, his rear in the air, then—one at a time—his back legs. Then he shakes himself and starts up the driveway after her, prancing and smiling. After a moment he passes her. Tail waving, he trots ahead down the road toward the woods trail, pausing now and again to look back over his shoulder to be sure she is coming.

The next day, before she gives him his breakfast,

Charley takes him for a walk. And there is a new pattern.

They go every day, no matter what the weather is like. Because there is no particular destination on these walks, Charley lets Coyote choose where they will go. It is quickly clear that he knows the woods better than she does. He takes her on old logging roads, ATV trails, side branches of the sewer line access. Though he doesn't need to follow trails, he seems to understand that she does. Or maybe he, too, likes the way cleared of brambles and honeysuckle. After they've walked for a while, he goes off cross-country on his own, but no matter how far she walks, whether she turns back on the same trail or off on another one, he always manages to find her again.

If she doesn't see him for such a long time that she starts worrying about roads again, and cars, she whistles for him. Sometimes he actually comes. Once in a while Sadie comes to the whistle instead, and finishes the walk with her. With or without Sadie, by the time Charley gets home again, Coyote is always with her. Once, when she thinks he is behind her, she waits and waits by the chain across the end of the road for him to catch up. When she finally gives up and goes home, she finds Coyote sitting at the head of the driveway, waiting for her. "What took you so long?" his expression says. "Where's my breakfast?"

With no place special to go, Charley isn't in a hurry. She walks slowly and finds herself noticing things she hasn't noticed before. Once she spends fifteen minutes trying to follow a line of ants carrying things, looking like bearers on safari. Moving their colony, she thinks. It's easy enough to discover where they are coming from, a hole beneath a tree, but try as she might she never finds where they are going. The line just seems to peter out in the leaf litter. She sees a woodpecker disappear into a hole in a dead tree and wonders if it is feeding young ones. Hearing a hawk scream overhead one day, she looks up and sees an enormous chunk of broken tree hanging above her, one end caught among the branches of another tree, the other moving slightly in the light wind. She scuttles out from under it and then realizes it is very old, is rotting slowly away in the air. It has probably been hanging there that way since Hurricane Hugo.

There's so much death in these woods, she thinks, noticing how many blowdowns she can see standing where she is. *And so much life*, a voice sounds in her head. Yes, she answers, listening to a woodpecker's laughing call.

Coyote likes going up the sewer line access toward where Dixie Trace, the new housing development, is going in. Even though ATVs have beaten a path, blackberry brambles grow thickly on both sides, up the hill from where the lake trail angles off. They are half-choked with honeysuckle vines, but there are plenty of berries. And plenty of thorns. The thorns are so wicked that Charley can't pick berries without getting scratched and bloody, but the berries are worth it, shiny and fat and sweet.

Along this trail, wide enough to be sunny most of the day, there are huge, circular spiderwebs with gigantic green and yellow and black spiders sitting in the middle, their legs spread out to feel vibrations in the strands. On a foggy morning Charley finds a web lined with drops of water like pearls and wishes she had a camera, wishes she knew how to do what her mother did. She stands for a long time, trying to burn the image into her brain so it will stay with her, even though she can't bring it back, capture it on paper, and frame it.

On Day Thirty-eight of The Taming, with Coyote as her guide, she finds the way from the sewer line access, across the creek behind the new housing development, and up the power lines all the way around the lake to the Dumpster on the road that leads in through the gates—where she saw him as a wild thing that very first time before the accident. The power company keeps the trees cut beneath the lines, so the way is mostly tall grass and wildflowers, blackberry brambles and pine saplings—like an overgrown Christmas tree farm, Charley thinks. The ATVs have been here, too, leaving deep red clay ruts through the weeds. That day Charley doesn't get home till nearly noon, and Sarita meets her at the door, furious. "You let me know before you leave if you're planning to walk to China and back!"

Charley, hungry, soaked with sweat, and limping more than usual, holds out a plastic grocery bag, heavy with blackberries. The berries cool Sarita's temper, but Charley can't decide what made her so mad—whether she was worried about Charley or only about what Paul Morgan would say if something happened to his daughter when she was being paid to watch her.

Later, when they are eating the blackberry muffins Sarita has made, she tells Charley she was so worried that she gave up working on her puzzle. "I was picturing you at the bottom of a cliff someplace, smashed to pieces. Or drowned."

"Don't worry about me drowning," Charley says. "I don't go in the lake."

Sarita slathers butter on a muffin. "I've been meaning to mention what a waste that is, girl. Here you are living on a lake with three swim docks and the cleanest water in the county. Swimming's good exercise."

"I don't see you swimming Eagle Lake every day," Charley says.

"You won't, either—all those snakes and snapping turtles."

Charley nods. After two years of Amy's pool, the clear blue water with nothing in it you can't see, it gives her the creeps, too, to think what would be swimming with her in the lake. But that wasn't always true.

Charley learned to swim in Eagle Lake. She knows perfectly well that the turtles and the shy brown water snakes that sometimes zigzag across the surface want no more to do with a swimmer than the swimmer wants to do with them. She and her mother and her father used to swim—all three of them together—every evening when her father got home from work. He didn't used to go back to the office after dinner, which in good weather they mostly ate outside on the terrace. The dock box is still full of swim noodles and fins and goggles and inflatable toys. She and her father don't use them anymore. Maybe, Charley thinks. Maybe someday.

16

The Pine Grove

Sarita comes in from her drive up to the mailboxes and hands Charley a letter from Amy. Charley can feel Sarita's eyes on her back as she starts for the kitchen to throw it away. She can imagine the look on Sarita's face—the same look she gets when Charley refuses an invitation to hang out with the kids from school. Sarita probably thinks, like Charley's father does, that she shouldn't be alone so much, that she should be going out with friends, having them over to the house.

But Charley doesn't want to leave Coyote—not yet—and she certainly doesn't want a bunch of kids coming around and scaring him into the woods. Besides, there's something else, something almost magical happening this summer that she can't explain, even to herself. It isn't something she wants to share.

Still aware of Sarita watching, Charley doesn't drop Amy's letter in the trash this time. She goes to her room instead, sticks the letter, unopened, in the frame of her mirror, and flops onto her bed. It is July 18. The red number on the calendar today is 39. The summer is more than half gone. One month from today, school starts again. Amy will come home from up north, and Charley will have to go back to school. What will happen then?

She doesn't want to think about it. Doesn't want to think about Amy. Amy's probably only writing because she feels guilty. She *ought* to feel guilty, going away and—

Charley stops in the middle of the thought. It is just a habit, she realizes, grumping about Amy and Becky Sue, Lake George and tennis. She is surprised to find that she isn't angry anymore. Whatever Amy is doing this summer, there is no wild dog in it. Whatever Amy is doing, Charley is having a better summer. She grins and gets up. She will take some biscuits outside for the dogs.

The next morning Coyote leads Charley back up the sewer line access trail. Maybe, she thinks, he's hoping she will be willing to do the whole power line hike again and stay out all morning. It's Saturday, Sarita's day off, so she could. Today her father won't wait till she gets back to go to the office. He's decided she can take care of herself for a few hours. But it's only eight in the morning and already the sun is beating down on the trail so hard that she really wants to get off it and into the shade. Under the power lines there is no shade at all.

She looks to see where Coyote has gone. He's disappeared. Her choice is to turn back and take the lake trail, hoping he'll figure out where she's gone and come find her, or cut into the woods where there isn't a trail. Her leg isn't hurting too badly, and she feels up for adventure, so she decides to cut into the woods. On her left the ground slopes down toward Heron Pond and gets marshy. Once she pushes her way through the screen of honeysuckle and poison ivy and blackberries to get in under the trees, the walking will be bad. On her right the ground slopes up. The sun has encouraged pretty much the same tangle of undergrowth among the pine and sweet gum saplings on both sides, so whichever she chooses, the going won't be easy at first. But at least to the right there won't be mud.

She keeps walking, looking for a break in the undergrowth, until she sees, through a stand of tall pine saplings, what looks like a clearing of reddish sand. There seems to be nothing growing there, and she wonders if it could really be sand, here where all the soil is heavy

Carolina clay. She remembers, then, a winter photo her mother took of a place where sand and water have frozen into a forest of tiny stalagmites. This must be that place. The blackberry brambles have petered out along the edges of the trail, leaving only honeysuckle and a wild rose, its wickedly barbed branches spraying out like a fountain. Amazing, Charley thinks, how many things in nature have thorns. Skirting the rosebush, she heads in toward the clearing, pushing pine boughs out of the way, ducking under or stepping over vines.

Whatever made this clearing, it is floored with coarse, sandy soil, lighter than the color of the clay. It slopes up to a wooded hill, covered with moss and pine needles. In the middle of the clearing there is a small pile of black dung, studded with seeds. *Scat*, her mother called these leavings of the woods animals. It is one way to track the animals. Charley has no idea what left it— raccoon or possum or maybe a fox.

She crosses the clearing and climbs the hill, holding onto the trunks of young pines and cedars to pull herself up. When she gets to the top, she recognizes it immediately. She has found the Pine Grove.

Pines and cedars grow so tall and so dense here that the shade is too deep for undergrowth. The lower branches of the trees have died and mostly broken away, leaving clear space for standing. She can look in any direction and see what seem to be corridors of tree trunks—some straight, some curving down the slopes. The place where she is standing now, a rounded knoll, is an almost perfect circle, like a green-roofed room with a mossy floor where the fairy rings grow. There is no sign of mushrooms now. It is dim and still here, almost cool. Unlike the ground everywhere else in the woods, there are no leaves. A scattering of sharp-edged white stones peek out from the carpet of pine needles, moss, and lichens that covers the ground.

It feels as if she has stepped from the bright, hot summer of Eagle Lake into a different season, a different world. She finds herself breathing more deeply, taking in the sharp scent of pine sap and cedar. If she could feel her heartbeat, she thinks, it would be slowing down. This is a place she does not want to leave.

She lowers herself to the ground and leans against the trunk of a pine, her left leg tucked up under her, her right stretched out in front. The stillness settles around her. Gradually she becomes aware of insects buzzing. The twittering of birds. And there is something else, something that isn't quite a sound. It is more like a vibration, as if the pine grove and the woods beyond are breathing in time with her breath.

What you hear depends on how you listen. The thought appears in her mind and hovers there, like a humming-bird at the feeders her mother used to put out. *What you hear depends on how you listen.* She sits as still as she can, aware of the birds, the insects, the breathing of the woods. Her eyes focus on the feathery branches of a cedar on the other side of the knoll, then on the thick-plated bark of a pine. There is a quick glimmer of silver light. She shifts her focus and sees a fine line of gossamer trailing across the clearing. One of the lines of web a spider stick catches, she thinks. The kind she can't see. Maybe she has not been looking the right way.

She doesn't know how long she stays, drifting in the stillness, before the shrill voice of a blue jay in the top of a nearby tree jolts her back to herself.

Where is Coyote? She whistles once, then again. Will he find her here, in this place they've never come to before, or will he expect her to be on the trail some-where, heading home? She doesn't want to move yet, doesn't want to leave this place. She will wait for a while and see if he will come.

Where is he? she wonders again. What is he doing? She closes her eyes, and an image forms of him sniffing around the base of a tree stump, scenting something burrowed underneath. He digs with his front paws, throwing clots of red clay out behind him. When he can't get to the animal he is after, he sets off, trotting through the woods, ducking under bushes and jumping over fallen trees. Then she imagines him stopping, ears and nose twitching. He has caught the scent of a deer. There are plenty of deer in the woods, Charley knows, though they aren't very often seen in the daytime. Sometimes at dusk they come out under the power lines or into the field near Eagle Lake's stone gates. From time to time she has noticed hoofprints in the mud by the ponds.

Now she sees a pair of deer, a doe and a young buck, leaping up from where they have been sheltering in a hollow beneath a fallen tree. They leap away, and Coyote takes off after them, becoming a golden blur, running and jumping and swerving among the trees. They splash through a creek and up the bank on the other side, Coyote behind them. Then they angle to the left, and Coyote cuts across a small clearing, closing the distance between them. He leaps at the one that is lagging slightly behind, and it kicks, its hoof catching Coyote across the bridge of his nose. Coyote yelps and stops as the deer goes on, bounding over a fallen pine tree and disappearing into the brush. Panting hard, Coyote watches it go. There is a sharp, curved line of blood across his nose where the deer's hoof connected.

Charley shakes her head and opens her eyes. Wherever Coyote is, it is time to start back. Her legs are stiff, and she can feel where the bark of the pine tree she's been leaning against has left a pattern on her back. She pushes herself to her feet, stretches her arms over her head, circles her shoulders a couple of times, and heads down the hill into the sandy clearing, holding to the trees to slow her progress. She will be coming back to the Pine Grove, she thinks. It is a perfect place to rest while Coyote does whatever he does in the woods.

The sun is hotter than ever out on the trail, and she is eager to get home and change out of her jeans. From time to time as she walks, she whistles for Coyote. The blackberries are almost gone now, but she snatches a late one and pops it into her mouth. It is dry and hot and not good. She has just passed the cutoff to the lake trail when Coyote comes down out of the woods on the other side.

"Well, it's about time," she says. "You're a mess!" His legs are muddy, his fur is studded with clumps of red clay. Charley catches her breath. There is something else—a sharp, curved line of blood across his nose.

17

Touch

Hot as it is, the rest of the way home Charley is aware of a chill up her back and along her shoulders. The cut on Coyote's nose is exactly the way she saw it. Did he really chase a pair of deer? Did he splash through a creek and leap at a deer who kicked him and got away?

There is no doubt about the cut, about the blood on his nose.

All this time she's been imagining things about Coyote, she's had no way to be sure whether what she sees in her mind is real or not. She only knows how real it has *felt*. This is different. She saw that cut, saw it happen in her mind, before she saw it with her eyes.

She wants to tell someone about this. But who can

she tell? Her father won't believe her. He used to complain about how long her mother encouraged her fantasies of fairies in the woods. "The sooner she knows the difference between what's real and what's not, the better!" This is real, though. It is.

She could tell Sarita, but she has no idea what Sarita would think about it. Besides, Sarita might tell Charley's father.

At home she feeds Coyote, wishing that she could put some sort of medicine on his nose. The cut is crusting over, but it looks deep. It's possible that the fur won't grow back and he'll have a scar the rest of his life. It doesn't seem to bother him, though. He doesn't paw at it, doesn't shake his head as if it hurts. Or maybe he's had enough pain that he's used to it. Like Charley and her leg.

Charley goes to her room to change her clothes, her mind still reeling. She strips off her jeans and T-shirt, checks for ticks, drapes the clothes over a chair to dry out, and sits on her bed in her underwear. She closes her eyes. Can she make an image of Coyote now? Of course. She can see him perfectly clearly in her mind, lying under the dogwood. But he always goes there after breakfast if Sadie isn't around. This isn't what she did in the Pine Grove.

Charley shifts to Sadie, lets a picture form in her mind of Sadie swimming across the lake, making splashes with her front paws. Clearly as she can see it, it isn't the same as the deer chasing, either. She has seen Sadie do this so often that the image she is seeing in her mind now is ordinary memory. Even if she were to go outside right this minute and find Sadie coming up out of the water and shaking herself, it wouldn't prove anything. Sadie swims over at this time of day a lot.

In the Pine Grove she was just playing with the images, drifting. She wasn't making a real effort to see what Coyote was doing. Does that make a difference? Now it's like a test, to see if she can do it again. Now there is something to prove.

If Amy were here, Charley thinks, and still her best friend, she could tell her. Amy would think it was cool. Weird—a little scary—but really, really cool. Charley grins. Whether Amy would think that or not, she does. Definitely. Weird—a little scary—but *really, really cool*!

The corner of her mother's book is sticking out from under the extra pillow. Her mother—that's who Charley wants to tell about this. Colleen Morgan wouldn't refuse to believe her or tell her she's crazy. But Colleen Morgan isn't here. And she never will be.

Charley pulls the book out and finds the page with

the fairy ring. There, scattered in the moss and pine needles in the middle of the circle of mushrooms, are the
same white stones she saw today. Except for the mushrooms, the Pine Grove looks today the way it did when
her mother was kneeling in it, taking the picture.
Looking at it makes Charley's throat hurt. She turns the
page.

The next photo is of Eagle Lake, taken from the dam
on a soft, gray morning, tendrils of silvery mist like
whirlpools rising from the surface of the water. "'The
real voyage of discovery consists not in seeking new landscapes, but in having new eyes.'—Marcel Proust."

New eyes. Like when she looked across the Pine
Grove and saw the strand of spiderweb. It occurs to
Charley that her mother saw the lake and the woods
around it differently than anyone else who lives here.
What she saw she captured, and then she sent the images
out into the world for other people to share.

The next page is a single white wildflower, incredibly
close-up, with five petals arranged around a spray of
golden dots. There is nothing else in the picture—just
the flower against a dark background, green but un-
focused. "'Nobody sees a flower—really—it is so small it
takes time—we haven't time—and to see takes time, like
to have a friend takes time.'—Georgia O'Keeffe."

And then there is the beaver again. "To understand any living thing you must creep within and feel the beating of its heart." Is that what her mother could do? Did she connect with the animals spirit to spirit? Is that why she never needed to make a blind to get her photographs?

Charley's throat is hurting again. She closes the book and puts it back. Then she gets dressed and goes outside. Sadie and Coyote are chasing each other around the azaleas. Sadie is wet from swimming the lake. Of course she is. It doesn't mean a thing.

A few hours later, when Charley has finished a cheese sandwich that she shared with the dogs—Coyote coming close enough to take his share from her hand—the dogs are playing again. They roll on their backs next to each other, biting at each other's ears and paws whenever they get close enough. Charley goes over and sits down next to Sadie, expecting Coyote to leap up and move away. He doesn't. The two dogs keep snapping at each other, gently, not really trying to connect, and Charley rubs Sadie's stomach.

After a minute she reaches over Sadie and gingerly lays her hand on Coyote's chest. He looks up at her, and their eyes lock. He has registered this touch, knows it is her hand on his chest. *Good dog,* she thinks. Holding her breath, she begins to rub. Coyote wriggles in the grass just the way Sadie was doing a moment ago. After a while he rolls onto his side, away from her. She rubs behind his ears and then runs her hand through the honey-gold fur down his back to the base of his tail. His fur is wavy and a little wiry, not as soft as Sadie's. If she had ointment to put on the cut on his nose, she could do it now, he is so relaxed. His tail thumps on the ground once, twice—and then Sadie jumps up and knocks Charley sideways. The moment is gone. The two dogs take off again, Coyote ducking in among the azaleas to leap out at Sadie as she runs past.

Charley sits there, her hand tingling. She has touched Coyote. Petted him. Forty days it has taken her—longer than she could ever have guessed when she got the idea to invite Coyote to live with them. People take this for granted, she thinks, this petting of dogs. As if this is what dogs are *for*.

She has touched Coyote, rubbed his ears. Like Jane Goodall grooming a wild chimpanzee for the first time. Charley knows, now, how that must have felt, what it must have meant.

18

Regular Dog

The next day Charley wakes with the memory of Coyote's fur under her hand and hurries to dress, wondering, now that Coyote has allowed her to pet him, what will be different today.

But there has been no breakthrough, no miraculous change. All through the walk and the feeding, Coyote stays well out of her reach, seeming, if anything, even more wary than usual. It is Sunday. Sadie, probably chained while the Davises are at church, doesn't swim across the lake. Without her, Coyote refuses to come close enough even to take a piece of liver from Charley's hand. It is as if yesterday never happened.

When Sarita gets back from church, Charley is sitting, near tears, at the breakfast table in the lake room.

Her father is alternating between watching a Sunday morning news program and reading the newspaper. "What's wrong?" Sarita asks the moment she sees the look on Charley's face.

"Nothing," Charley says.

"Some nothing." Sarita sets to work in the kitchen, putting out the ingredients for the waffles she always fixes for Sunday brunch. She pours a glass of lemonade and sets it on the counter that separates the kitchen from the lake room. "Maybe this'll help."

Surprisingly, it does. As she drinks, Charley watches one squirrel chase another, leaping from branch to branch outside the floor-to-ceiling windows. Nothing can take away what happened yesterday, she thinks. Maybe the connection scared Coyote, and he needs to back off a little. Like the first time she got up the nerve to dive off the swim platform. It was days and days before she dared to do it again. But a few weeks later, diving was the most natural thing in the world.

Over brunch, Charley tells her father about petting Coyote.

"Terrific! It's time to get a collar on him," he says. "And take him to a vet. I'd have insisted on that from the start, but I didn't really expect him to stick around."

"He'll stay," Charley says. "This is his territory now."

But her heart sinks at the thought of putting a collar on him, leashing him, forcing him into a car to take him to a vet. It will feel to him, she thinks, like the men catching him and putting him in the shed. "I don't see how we can get him to a vet, though."

"Sorry, kiddo, but there's no choice." Her father takes another waffle from the platter Sarita has brought to the table. "If you're going to keep this dog, he has to have his shots. Distemper, rabies—especially rabies. There's a law. And who knows what else he might need? I doubt he's been neutered, for instance. We'll have to have that done, too."

"There's a sign for a mobile vet on the road by the police academy," Sarita says. "You could call."

"Good idea," Paul Morgan says. "You call and make the arrangements, Charley, and I'll pay for it." He sighs. "Another of the truths of life. There is no such thing as a free dog!"

Much as Charley likes waffles, she has lost her appetite. How is she going to get a collar on Coyote? And if she does, what will happen when she turns him over to a vet—a person he doesn't know who will stick needles in him? At least shots can be given at home. Neutering will mean taking him to the vet's office. Car, strange place, operation, pain, car. Worse than being locked in a shed. Much worse. It's too horrible to think about. Coyote will never trust her again. He'll probably take off and never come back.

When Charley is helping in the kitchen later, Sarita pats her arm. "That dog's life is so much better than he ever had before, he's not going to leave just because you put a collar on him."

"I don't even know if I *can* put a collar on him."

"Huh!" Sarita says nothing more. She just goes on rinsing dishes and putting them in the dishwasher, humming to herself.

Maybe, Charley thinks, the mobile vet has tranquilizer darts like the ones they use on wild animals. Coyote wouldn't even remember what had happened to him when he woke up. Of course, to use a tranquilizer dart, the vet would have to be able to shoot him with it. If a stranger drives up to the house, Coyote will be gone in less time than it takes the vet to get out of the car.

By Wednesday Coyote is taking liver from her hand, whether Sadie is around or not. Charley takes him a piece several times in the morning and several more in the afternoon. She just calls, "Liver!" and wherever he is, he comes to get it. If Sadie is there, of course, she has to give some to her, too, but Sarita has filled the freezer with enough to feed an army of dogs. Charley's hoping that when Coyote's used to coming for liver, she'll be able to get the collar on him.

Unfortunately, he doesn't come close enough. He stands back and takes the liver the way he takes food from his bowl, leaning forward, snatching it, and jumping back so fast she can't possibly even touch him, let alone catch him.

She tries using Sadie. If Sadie doesn't come over on her own, Charley goes down to the dock and calls across the lake for her. Then, when the dogs are playing, Charley joins them. Coyote lets her get close enough to pet him. It's clear that he's doing it on purpose. He lets her take burrs off his coat, and she is finally able to pull the snarls and tangles out of his tail. Eventually he even lets her take hold of the ruff around his neck—exactly what she has to do to put the collar on him.

Except when she has the collar. The minute she comes out of the house with the collar in her hand, he scoots away and stays away, no matter what. She tries putting the collar in her pocket before she comes out. It makes no difference. If she has the collar, even if Coyote can't see it, he stays away. She can play with Sadie all she wants. He just stands and watches.

Then, if she leaves the collar inside, he comes with

Sadie and lets Charley pet him. She can't figure out how he knows when she has it. Sarita says maybe he smells it. So Charley rubs it all over with liver. It doesn't help.

Finally she enlists Sarita. "You be ready with the collar in the house, and when I'm close enough to get hold of him, bring it out to me."

Even that doesn't work. Charley might as well have been waving it around in the air and telling him she's going to put it on him. He refuses to come near her. She decides that the dog is reading her mind. It's the only explanation that makes sense. Even when she doesn't have the collar, if she's *planning* to catch him, he knows it.

"Uncanny," her father says, though he doesn't believe in psychic dogs. He is getting impatient. "One way or another, you need to get control of that dog."

It is then that Charley decides to *tell* Coyote what is going on. Maybe the trouble is that she's trying to trick him. Somehow he knows that's what she's doing. And Coyote doesn't like to be tricked.

That is how she ends up sitting on a boulder at the shallow end of the lake during their walk that misty Thursday morning, the forty-fifth day of The Taming, talking to Coyote.

Ever since the day at the Pine Grove, she has managed to find a place to sit during their morning walk—on a stump or a fallen tree or a boulder. Coyote goes off and does whatever it is he does, and she waits for him to come back. She doesn't get bored by this wait, the way she used to in the evenings over by the Heywards'. What she does now is listen. There are more things to hear in the woods than she ever would have believed. Sometimes she thinks she can hear the sap moving in the trees, beetles chewing their way through the bark. Once a movement catches her eye, and she looks up in time to see an owl, its huge wings moving slowly, silently, fly off between the trees. It makes no sound, but she can almost feel the currents of air from its wings.

Occasionally, when she is relaxed enough, she plays with visualizing what Coyote is doing. She sees him chase a squirrel or pounce into the leaves, trying to catch whatever small thing—a mouse or a vole, maybe—he has heard rustling beneath.

The more she does this, the clearer her images become. Sometimes, instead of watching him, it almost seems that she is right there with him, doing what he is doing. She can feel the pounding of his feet against the ground as he runs, the brush of leaves and grass against his face. From time to time she catches a whiff of something she doesn't recognize, smells that seem to start her heart racing. But if she tries too hard at this imagining, the images and feelings slip away and she is back to herself, sitting in the woods, alone and waiting.

This morning, when Coyote comes back to get the treats she usually gives him from her waist pack, she doesn't give them to him right away. He stands for a while, looking at her with an expression that seems to ask what the heck she is waiting for. After a while he sits. Finally, with a big, obvious sigh, he lies down with his chin on his paws, looking out at the water.

"Here's the thing," Charley says to him. His ears flick back toward her. "Dogs who live with people wear collars. It shows that they have a home and a family that cares about them. Sadie has one. And Beau and Pandy and Jasmine and Bernie—all the dogs at Eagle Lake. All except you. I promised you food and shelter, and I'm doing my best to keep my promise. But you need to wear a collar. I won't use it to make you do stuff you don't want to do."

Coyote still looks out at the lake, but his ears twitch. Charley realizes that isn't exactly the truth. "Well, *sometimes* I will, but only if it's absolutely necessary and only if it's for your own good. Like when a doctor comes to see you. There's a law, and there's nothing I can do about it. You need a shot—a couple of shots—to keep you from getting sick. And there are some other things we need to do if you're going to be safe and healthy and live with us the way dogs live with people. You want to be a regular dog, don't you?"

Coyote doesn't move. Charley wonders if she's crazy, telling him all this. "So when Sadie comes over today, I'm going to bring the collar outside, and I need you to let me put it on you. Okay? Coyote?"

Coyote gets up and stretches, front legs and then back. He shakes himself and looks up at her, his black-brown eyes gleaming in his golden face, the blue tip of his tongue visible between his teeth.

"Yeah, yeah, I know," she says. "You want your liver." She takes a piece of liver from her waist pack. "Are you going to let me put the collar on you?" His eyes are focused on the liver, his tail wagging. "I'm counting that wag as a promise!"

When Sadie swims over later that day, Charley tells her that she needs help. She explains about the collar, the shots. If Coyote can read human minds, maybe Sadie can, too.

Then she goes inside and gets the green nylon collar she chose for him so long ago. Holding it where both dogs can see it, she calls Sadie to her, rubs her ears, and pats her. Then she takes hold of Sadie's collar. "See?" she says to Coyote, who is standing just out of reach. "This is hers." She holds up the green one. "This is yours. We'll get a tag for it that has your name and phone number on it, just like Sadie has."

She lets go of Sadie's collar and rubs her ears some more. Coyote comes closer, close enough to touch. Slowly Charley moves her hand from Sadie to Coyote and rubs his ears. Then she takes a handful of his neck ruff and holds him while she puts the collar around his neck. His ears go back against his head and his tail droops, but he stands still while she buckles it on, making sure she can put two fingers between the collar and his neck. Then she lets him go and he backs quickly away, shaking his head.

Figuring it is better to leave him alone to get used to it, Charley goes inside. Sarita is standing at the dining room window. They stand together, watching Sadie circle Coyote, begging him to play. Moments later, collar forgotten, Coyote is chasing Sadie around the yard.

19

Survivor

Dr. Frazier, the mobile vet, doesn't have tranquilizer darts, he tells Charley when she calls, but he can send her a pill to give Coyote in a piece of liverwurst. If she gives it an hour before he's due to arrive, Coyote will get dopey enough that it will be easy to put a leash on him. "You won't even have to get him in the house. I'll do the checkup and take some blood and give him his shots right there in the yard. It should only take a few minutes. By the time he's feeling like himself again, I'll be gone and he won't even remember I was there." Charley likes the sound of his voice, likes it that he wants to be sure Coyote isn't traumatized. "You're doing a good thing," he tells her before he hangs up. "Difficult, but good." Charley grins. Let him tell Mr. Heyward that!

It is early on Monday, the forty-ninth day, when Charley takes the pill to Coyote, embedded in a piece of liverwurst. The vet is due at nine, so she has been up since seven. They have already had their walk, and Coyote has eaten. "This has a pill in it that will make you sleepy," she tells him. She doesn't want him to sense she is trying to trick him, or he might not come to get the liverwurst. She holds it out. "The vet is coming in a while to give you the shots I told you about. The pill will make it easier. He says you probably won't even remember after."

Coyote gulps the liverwurst and backs away. For a moment Charley is afraid that he might go off into the woods before the pill works, and she won't be able to find him. But he goes to his usual place under the dogwood and lies down.

Forty minutes later he is sleeping when she takes the green nylon leash outside. She has called Mrs. Davis and asked her to keep Sadie on their side of the lake today. As she approaches him, Coyote opens his eyes and tries to get up, but his feet slide out from under him. She can see in his eyes that this frightens him. "I'm sorry," she says as she clips the leash to his collar. "But it'll be okay. Really." She sits on the ground next to him and stays beside him, stroking him occasionally, until the vet arrives. When the van turns into the drive, Coyote struggles to his feet and tries to run, but he can't control his legs and quickly sinks back to the ground.

Dr. Frazier, a pudgy, smiley man with a shock of unruly red hair, turns out to be as quick and efficient as he is kind. It is all over, as he promised, in a few minutes. "He's a healthy, handsome dog," he tells her as he removes the cloth muzzle he has put on "just to be safe," and pats Coyote on the head. "Chow and shepherd, probably—about two years old, I'd say. You can take the leash off now and let him sleep the tranquilizer off. He'll be fine in a few hours."

At the door of his van, he turns back. "I'll give you a call when the lab work's done. Then we can talk about what else he might need."

Coyote stays dopey and confused, wobbling when he tries to walk, till the middle of the afternoon, and Charley feels like a traitor. But she puts the rabies tag on his collar, feeling a sense of real triumph. Coyote is legal now, officially a member of the Morgan family, a connection that will be recorded by the county.

It is Day Fifty and Coyote is completely back to normal when Dr. Frazier calls. "Listen now, Charley," he says when Sarita hands her the phone, "I don't want you to get upset." A chill runs through her. He wouldn't warn her if the news was good. "Coyote has heartworms." Heartworms, Charley thinks. She's heard of heartworms. They *kill* dogs! She wants to put down the phone, leave the room, stop this conversation.

"You're not to worry," the vet says in his hearty, cheery voice. "We can treat him. It's not the pleasantest treatment in the world, and it takes a long time, but he's a survivor. He's proved that. And he's young and healthy. I'm sure he'll come through just fine. We can do the whole thing there at the house. The only problem with this dog will be keeping him quiet after the treatments."

Keeping him quiet! "How'll we do that? He chases squirrels and deer, and he won't come in the house."

There is a pause. Charley can feel her heart pounding. "We don't want to wait too long, but we can wait a month or so to start the treatment. You can keep working on taming him. One way or another, we'll manage."

Charley takes a long, shaky breath. "So this treatment is all he needs?"

"Except for neutering. We won't be doing that until we're sure he's free and clear of worms—about a year from now. Remember, Charley, he's a survivor."

Later, when Charley tells her father, he shakes his head. "I'm sorry, kiddo. That's rough. But if the vet says the dog's healthy enough to survive the treatment, you can probably take his word."

She is afraid when she tells him how much the treatment will cost, he'll refuse. But he only sighs. "I told you there was no such thing as a free dog. We could take a week's vacation for that kind of money!"

As if Paul Morgan would ever take a vacation, Charley thinks. Sarita calls from the kitchen, "A week! That dog's given Charley the whole summer so far! Seems worth it to me!" It is the first time Sarita has ever offered an opinion on anything.

"All right, all right. I never said he wasn't worth it!" Her father reaches over to pat Charley's arm. "Don't worry. If this dog wasn't a survivor, he wouldn't have made it this long."

Charley wakes up the next day with the image of Tree in her mind. *Survivor*, she thinks. What she wants to do today is visit Tree. She doesn't know how to find him from the trail, but he's easy enough to see from the water.

Instead of putting on her hiking clothes, she dresses in shorts and sandals and tells Sarita she is going out in the canoe. Then she clips on her waist pack with biscuits and liver pieces in it, and goes outside to call Coyote, who is lying at the end of the driveway. He comes down the drive all smiles and wags and prance, his collar and tag jingling, and stops just far enough away that she can't touch him. "We're having a boat walk today," Charley says. At the word *walk* he starts frisking and bouncing, giving little yelp-barks as he heads back up toward the road. "No!" she calls. "*Boat* walk. Come this way!"

She walks around the house and down the gravel path toward the dock. Coyote follows, his tail only half-wagging, keeping his distance. This is not the pattern he's used to. "It's still a walk," she tells him. "Except that I'm going in the boat, and you're going on land." She isn't sure this will work, but it's worth a try.

Her mother's green canoe, the name *Dragonfly* painted on its bow, is upside-down on the bank, where it has lain untouched for two years. Remembering Mrs. Sutcliff's story about finding a snake under her canoe, Charley flips the boat gingerly, leaping back as it goes over. There is no snake under it, and nothing in it but spiders. From the dock box she gets a paddle and two swim noodles to take along as emergency flotation devices. Coyote is sitting at the top of the path to the dock, watching her warily.

Holding the bowline, Charley pushes the canoe down the slope of the hill into the lake, pulls it close, and steps in. Her leg gives a twinge as she pushes off, but the pain is so brief, it is easy to ignore. "Come on!" she calls to Coyote when she is settled. She paddles out into the water. "Follow me. Boat walk!" She angles to the right and heads around the bend to the shallow end of the lake. Coyote watches a while and then trots down to the edge of the lake and begins to follow, weaving through the trees and bushes along the shore.

When he reaches Mr. Garrison's yard, Coyote goes up for a visit with Jasmine and Bernie in their pen, all three of them running back and forth along the fence and barking. Then he runs back to see where Charley is, and follows her on past the last lot that has only a storage shed and a ramshackle dock.

Tree is directly across from this dock, but instead of paddling straight across the lake, Charley follows the shore so that Coyote can stay with her. He comes to the lake edge every so often to see where she is, but most of the time he is off on his own in the woods, just like on any other walk. At this end of the lake, it's easy to see where the original creek wound down into the gully that has become Eagle Lake. The water here is so shallow that Charley can see schools of minnows rushing back and forth over the bottom. Whirligig beetles circle and whirl on the surface of the water. The smell of rotted leaves and bottom muck rises with every sweep of the paddle.

Low bushes grow out into the marshy shallows on either side of the original creek bed.

Here Coyote cuts across from one side to the other, splashing through the water, weaving in and out among the bushes and then swimming the narrow stretch of deep water. It's the first time Charley has seen him swim willingly, and she suspects he didn't expect to step suddenly off into water too deep to touch bottom. On the other side, he shakes himself and runs up the hill under the trees, his legs caked with black bottom mud.

When Charley reaches Tree, Coyote is nowhere to be seen. She stops the canoe where her mother must have stopped to take the picture for the book jacket and lets the canoe drift. There is a light breeze stirring up the water so that the reflection of Tree's leaves, green now instead of red, is not like in the photograph. The breeze keeps the canoe moving and Charley wonders how, even on a day with no wind, her mother managed to hold the canoe still enough to take the picture.

She paddles toward Tree, and the canoe hangs up on a limb that has fallen into the water. It takes her a while to figure out how to maneuver around it. There is a tall, arch-shaped hole in the trunk where Tree stands in the water and she leans to take hold of the edge of the hole to pull the canoe in close. Poison ivy grows up one side of the trunk, and spiders have spun thick webs inside the hole. She can see layers of rotting wood and dark, still water inside, but all around the hole is the solid, living trunk, far too big for Charley to get her arms around.

When Charley was about eight years old, she remembers, her mother had her hold a dead stick in one hand and a long twig of a living tree in the other. "Feel the difference?" she asked. "Feel the life?"

Charley wasn't sure she felt it then, but she can feel it now, her hand on Tree's rough bark. *Hi!* Her mother talked to Tree, but she only thinks the greeting. She sits for a moment, aware of the sensation of life under her hand, the slight movement of the canoe, the breeze on her skin. And then it is as if Tree has answered. There are no words. It is more as if something old and completely friendly has welcomed her. Ants are running up and down the ridges in the bark. Charley wonders how many living things make their home in Tree. She wonders whether Tree likes having them there.

Almost immediately she realizes it is not about liking or not liking. *It's how it is.* That is her own thought, of course. But still, it feels like an answer.

From up the hill and farther around the lake, Coyote begins to bark—the high, light bark that means he's treed a squirrel and is hoping he can bark it back down. She wishes she could take some bit of this tree's spirit, whatever it is that keeps it alive in spite of the water, in spite of the hole and the spiders and the ants. Tree has what Coyote needs.

So does Coyote.

"I'll be back sometime," she says, aloud this time.

I'll be here.

20

Two Steps Forward

It is nine-thirty in the evening, the first of August, and a light rain is falling. Brief, blustery storms have alternated with this steady rain most of the long, boring day. Thunder rumbles occasionally in the distance. Sarita has gone to her room, Charley's father is watching a car chase movie on television, and Charley is stretched out in the recliner chair, her eyes closed, ignoring the movie and letting her mind drift. Coyote spent most of the day behind the boxwood hedge at the front of the house, lying against the bricks under the roof overhang out of the rain. It is the closest he has ever come to the house, and Charley considers it a huge step forward. He isn't there now, hasn't been since it got dark, but still, he purposely took shelter against the house.

She quiets her mind and lets images come to her of Coyote in the woods across the road. She can hear rain on the leaves overhead, smell the damp ground. She senses more than sees Coyote in the darkness, feeling the nest he has dug himself in the leaves beneath a shrub that leans over a tree stump. His back is against the stump, his nose under his tail. His fur is damp, but the dampness doesn't reach all the way down to his skin. He has not eaten, she knows, since breakfast this morning.

Charley opens her eyes and sits up. Coyote ought to have a bedtime snack, something more than a few pieces of liver in the afternoon to carry him through the night. Sarita has bought a box of big biscuits—for large dogs. One of those would be good. "I'm going out," she tells her father as she pushes herself out of the chair. "I'll be back in a few minutes."

"Where are you going? It's nearly ten o'clock!"

Charley points to the clock on the DVD player. "Nine forty-two. I'm going to take Coyote a bedtime snack."

"Do you know where he is?"

"Somewhere close," she says.

Outside the rain has dwindled to a heavy mist. The lights of the city, reflected by the clouds, give the gravel road a tone of pale gray against the deep shadows of the woods. She whistles and calls for Coyote. "I've got a biscuit. A big one!" Then she stands very still and listens. Distant thunder growls. Water drips from the trees.

She calls Coyote again, mentions the biscuit again. Nothing. She whistles two more times and is about to whistle again when she hears movement among the trees. She calls again. In a few moments a shape, pale in the darkness, materializes out of the trees. Coyote moves across the road and stands a few feet away, his tail waving. He has come when she called. Out of the woods. At night! "Good dog! I brought you a bedtime snack." She holds out the biscuit and says, "Sit," as she always does with Sadie.

He stands for a moment, looking up at her, and then, to her complete astonishment, he sits. She gives him the biscuit. He crunches down on it and pieces fall to the ground. He swallows the first bit, then stands up to get the others, picking them up from the road one at a time. When he has gotten the last crumbs, he doesn't immediately bolt back to the woods. Slowly and gently, Charley reaches to pat him on the head. He allows her to do this, his tail moving slightly.

Charley has an idea, suddenly. So radical is this idea that she stands for a moment, trying to decide whether it's even possible. Yes. It is. "Stick around," she says to

Coyote. "I'm going to get you some liver."

She turns and hurries back to the house, leaving Coyote at the edge of the road. Inside, she piles a handful of liver pieces onto a saucer. Then she changes into her sleep T-shirt and gathers sheets, a light blanket, and a pillow from the linen closet. "I'm trying an experiment," she tells her father as she heads for the stairs, the saucer of liver balanced on the pile of linens in her arms. "Sarita," she calls as she starts down, holding the railing and moving carefully to keep from dropping anything. "Is it okay if I come through your room?"

"Sure. What's up?" Sarita is in bed, reading.

"I'm going to spend the night in Mom's studio."

Sarita puts down her book. "You're going to what?"

"I'll explain tomorrow. Is it okay if I use your bathroom in the night?"

"Of course."

At the closed door of her mother's studio, Charley stops for a moment. Can she do this? Yes, she decides. Yes. It's the only way.

She turns on the light at the wall switch, closes the door behind her, and goes to the daybed under the farthest window. Setting down the liver, she dumps the linens on the floor and begins moving the boxes from the bed to the worktable, putting them on the floor underneath it. When she has spread the sheets and blankets on the bed and settled the pillow in place, she surveys the room, trying to see it through Coyote's eyes. Too bright. Charley turns on the desk lamp and switches off the overhead lights. Better.

Then she opens the outside door and the screen, slides the metal disk in place to keep the screen door propped open, and steps, barefoot, outside under the roof overhang. It is raining again, and lightning brightens the sky intermittently as thunder rumbles closer. The woods of the empty lot next door are dark against the sky.

"Coyote!" she calls up toward the road. "Coyote, *liver*!" She puts her fingers in her mouth and whistles, once, twice. Then she gets the liver and stands, watching and listening. "Liver! Come get some liver."

After a moment Charley hears, over the sound of the rain, the light jingle of the tag on Coyote's collar. He appears in the spill of soft light from the door, his ears down, rain dripping from his nose. "Liver," she says, holding a piece out to him. He looks at the house, his shoulders hunched, and then slowly, cautiously, moves forward and takes it from her fingers.

Charley backs through the open door and holds out another piece. "More," she says to him. "Come in and get it."

He stands in the rain and begins to whine. "It's okay. You can come in. It's dry in here."

Coyote whines again, but doesn't come. Charley is trying to decide whether to go back and give him another piece of liver outside, when lightning flashes blue-white, and thunder cracks. Coyote scuttles in through the door, snatches the liver from her hand, swallows, and then stands, shivering and looking around the dim, shadowy room. Charley discovers she is holding her breath. Coyote is inside the house. She is afraid to move, afraid he'll realize what he's done and scuttle back into the rain.

Lightning flashes again, and thunder follows almost immediately. The rain is pouring now. Coyote looks from Charley to the open door. She offers him another piece of liver, and he takes it. Still, she barely dares to breathe. She wants to go close the doors and keep him inside, dry and safe. But she knows what a closed door means to him, knows he would feel trapped, the way he was in that shed. She stands, watching, as he checks out the room, his eyes darting back to the open door again and again. "I won't close it," she tells him. "You can stay in or go out, whatever you want. If you want some more liver, you should sit."

He looks up at her and then sits. Piece by piece

Charley gives him the rest of the liver. When he has finished it, she holds her empty hands up to him. "All gone," she says.

After a moment Coyote lies down, facing the open door, his chin on his outstretched paws. "Good boy," Charley says. Moving slowly and carefully, she goes to the desk lamp and switches it off. Darkness closes in, so that now what little light there is comes from the sky outside. The rain continues steadily. Coyote stays where he is. Lightning flashes again, and she can see his form outlined against the open doorway. The thunder comes a moment later. The storm, Charley thinks, is moving away.

Slowly, so that she doesn't startle him, Charley gets into bed, pulling the covers up to her chin. The studio may get a little wet and a little buggy with the door open all night, she thinks. But Coyote is in the house.

Thank you, she thinks to the storm. If it hadn't been for the thunder and lightning, she doesn't know if this idea would have worked. But it did. It did. Two steps forward today, she thinks. This second step is such a big one she wants to shout in triumph. Coyote is *in the house.*

21

Amy

Charley wakes up twice during the night. Both times it is still raining. Both times she can make out Coyote's form lying on the floor, head toward the open door. The second time he is stretched out on his side, his tail out behind him, a picture of relaxation. It is too warm and muggy in the room to keep the blanket on. Charley drops it onto the floor and Coyote raises his head at the sound, looks at her for a moment, and then lies down again, with a deep sigh that seems to Charley to be a sigh of pure contentment. It is the most wonderful sound Charley has ever heard.

When she wakes again, the rain has stopped and weak sunlight is filtering through the trees of the lot next door, the wet leaves glittering like diamonds as they move in the morning breeze. Coyote is gone.

It's okay, Charley thought. He spent the night. And he knows now that he can do that and leave whenever he needs to. Someday, she is sure, she'll be able to invite him in and then close the door behind him. She'll be able to bring him in upstairs and he'll sleep in her room, at the foot of her bed. But for now this will do. For now she will sleep in the studio and let him come and go as he wants. She lies for a moment, looking at her mother's photographs on the walls. This is the Eagle Lake her mother saw, the Eagle Lake Charley is coming to know so well.

After breakfast, after the walk with Coyote, clouds move in again and it begins to rain. Coyote settles into his spot behind the boxwoods and Charley, with nothing else to do, takes her laptop to the breakfast table and turns it on. She checks her e-mail and watches the list of messages scroll onto the screen. There is the usual collection of spam and a few forwarded jokes from her friends.

The last message is from someone she doesn't know: "Skiguy5." And there's an attachment. She is about to delete it when she notices that the subject line says, "Hey, Charley!" Whoever it is, he knows her name. She clicks the symbol at the bottom of her screen to be sure her virus scan is on and opens the message.

Charley-O—

Don't freak, it's me, Amy. Skiguy5 is Adam, the club's waterskiing instructor who's letting me use his computer. He's cute, but really old—like 19.

Are you okay? Did you get my letters? How's your leg?

I am so sick of tennis I want to die. My arm hurts all the time. I'm probably getting tennis elbow and I'm not even any good! It's almost over, though. I'm coming home in just two more weeks!!!! School starts three days later—can you believe it?

Like I said in my letters, I am sorry for going away. *Really really* sorry! Becky Sue is okay, but she snores. And picks her nose when she thinks nobody's looking.

She has a totally awesome digital camera, though. I've been taking pictures like crazy, and Adam's burning them onto a CD for me so if you're speaking to me again by the time I get back, I'll show them to you. I'm thinking of join- ing the PhotoShop Club at school. I'm attaching my favorite picture.

Gotta go. Adam wants his computer. Just two more weeks. Don't be mad anymore, please!!!! Your friend—no matter what you think—Amy

Charley sits for a long moment, staring at the computer screen. "No matter what you think." She would have deleted this message if she had known who it was from. "How's your leg?" Charley realizes she hardly ever thinks about her leg these days. And she isn't mad at Amy anymore. But friends? So much has changed that she isn't sure what she feels now. Two more weeks. How can summer be over so soon?

She clicks on the JPEG attachment, and the photo appears on her screen. It's a picture of a tennis court with a silvery lake showing beyond it and pine-tree-covered mountains rising in the distance, but it's weirdly off center. So far to the left that she's almost out of the picture entirely, a girl she doesn't recognize is swinging a blurry racket. If this is supposed to be a picture of that girl, it's a waste. Charley is about to close it down when she notices that the figure sitting on a bench on the right, also almost out of the picture, is Becky Sue Lindner. She is dressed in a tennis outfit, holding a racket in one hand and picking her nose with the other. In spite of herself, Charley laughs out loud.

22

Time Together

*T*ime is suddenly getting away from her. With only two weeks until she will have to go to school, Charley decides she needs to spend more of every day with Coyote. Partly it's because the more they're together, the faster The Taming will go, and partly because she is already feeling how hard it will be to leave him for most of every day when school starts.

Charley has moved some of her things into the studio and sleeps there every night. Coyote spends the night with her most of the time. It gets humid and buggy with the screen door propped open, but whenever she tries to close it, he scurries out and won't come back. Charley's father says she can't just leave the door open indefinitely or the dampness could ruin everything in the studio, but she reminds him that she leaves it closed all day. "After a while he'll get used to being inside," she assures him, "and then I'll be able to close it."

In the mornings when she wakes up, Coyote has gone, and she finds him lying out at the end of the driveway when she goes outside. Then, on Day Sixty of The Taming, Charley opens her eyes to see him lying there still, the sun through the blinds making stripes on his golden fur. He raises his head to look at her. "Good morning," she says, and slowly sits up. He stays where he is, his tail thumping lightly on the floor. Gingerly, careful not to make any sudden moves, Charley slips out of bed onto her knees and reaches to pet him. He rolls over onto his side and lets her rub his chest. The connection Charley feels this time is like a steady vibration up through her arm and into her heart. This is more than a step forward, she thinks. Something very big has changed between them.

She tells Sarita about this when she goes upstairs, and is surprised to find herself blinking back tears.

Charley lets the morning walks become longer. The air is filled, these August days, with the thrum of cicadas, the chirp of crickets and katydids. She finds that she is listening with her eyes, her nose, her skin, as well as her ears. One day she feels a fly walking on her arm and watches as it stops and rubs its front feet together, then cleans its head, its iridescent blue-green body gleaming in the sun. She moves her arm, and it flies away. It was just an ordinary fly. If she could have gotten a picture of it in that moment before it flew, she wonders, would anyone else see how beautiful it was?

On August 9, the sixty-first day of The Taming, when they get around the shallow end of the lake and are heading home, Mrs. Davis and Jeremy and Bethanne are in the water by the swim raft, the kids in life jackets, Mrs. Davis on an inflatable chair with a glass of wine in the cup holder. Sadie is with them, splashing and barking. Charley watches the dog climb the ladder to the swim raft and jump off. No one has thrown something for her to retrieve. She just does it by herself.

Jeremy and Bethanne call to Charley to join them in the water. "Betcha you can't jump as far off the raft as I can," Jeremy says.

"I don't have my suit on," she tells them.

"And how long could it take to remedy that?" Mrs. Davis says, directing a splash at Charley's canoe. The spray of water feels marvelously cool.

"Come on!" Bethanne calls. "Go get your suit on and

come in and play with us."

Thinking about the feel of the water on her skin, Charley paddles across to her own dock, ties up the canoe, and goes inside to change. When she tells Sarita that she's going into the water, Sarita says she will come out and sit on the dock to watch.

"Some lifeguard you'll be," Charley says. "Scared of turtles and snakes."

"Then you'd better not need rescuing!" Sarita calls as Charley heads down the hall to her room.

When she gets back out to the dock, Coyote is sitting on the shore across the lake, watching Sadie leap off the swim raft, swim around it, and climb back up. "Insane," Charley imagines him saying, "retrievers are insane!"

Sarita comes down with a large glass of lemonade and a lawn chair and settles herself on the dock. Charley paddles the canoe out to the swim raft, ties it up, and climbs out.

"Eeewwww!" Jeremy says from the water when he sees the scar on her leg. "Did they have to cut your leg open to fix it?"

"It's a battle wound," Charley says. "My bone was sticking right out of my leg there, and they had to push it back in!"

"Gross!" Bethanne says. "Is that true?"

"It is," Charley says. It occurs to her that nothing that might be lurking in the water of Eagle Lake could possibly be worse than what she's been through. "Look out below!" she yells, and jumps into the water.

A new pattern is set that day. Walk, lunch, rest, boat walk, swim, dinner. Waiting and watching from the shore until everyone has finished swimming, Coyote is getting more and more used to being around humans.

Another change in Coyote has to do with Charley's father. Instead of hiding in the trees when Paul Morgan comes home, the dog has taken to going down the road to meet the car when he hears it coming, tail waving in welcome. He circles the car as it moves down the driveway and stays close when it stops, waiting for the door to open. He doesn't come close enough to be touched, but it's a greeting, nevertheless. Charley convinces her father to keep dog biscuits in the car and toss him one when he gets out, to encourage this behavior.

"He'll only like me for the biscuits," her father complains.

"Biscuits first, friendship after," Charley tells him. "One step at a time."

A week before school is due to start, Mr. Heyward

sees Charley and Coyote when they are walking near the mailboxes. "You've done a good job," he tells her. "He looks like a different animal."

"He is," she says. "He is."

23

Gone

Coyote is not in the studio when Charley wakes up the next morning. When she goes outside later, the driveway and the road are empty. Coyote is not waiting for her in his usual place. She swallows past a sudden sharpness in her throat. It's no big deal, she assures herself. He's probably just off in the woods. She whistles once, then again. He doesn't come. Maybe, she thinks, he has gone up to visit with Jasmine and Bernie.

She whistles several more times as she walks up the road. The two German shepherds are in their pen. Bernie barks a greeting. Coyote is nowhere to be seen. Now she is feeling a chill in the center of herself, somewhere under her rib cage.

She goes back into the house, where her father is

finishing his breakfast and Sarita is washing out the pan she used to fry bacon.

"He's probably off chasing something in the woods," her father says when she tells them. "He'll be back."

Sarita puts the pan into the dish drainer and dries her hands before she says anything. "Soon as he's hungry, that dog'll be back fussing at you to bring him some liver. Don't worry yourself."

Charley hates the casual tone they take. But she does her best to believe them. She goes to her room, sits on her bed, and closes her eyes to visualize the truth of where he is and what he's doing. In the first moments it seems to be a good idea. She feels him weaving his way through the woods, heading toward the sound of dogs barking. Charley has come to know the voices, the distinctive bark of most of the Eagle Lake dogs. This barking sounds like none of them. These dogs must be from one of the developments. As she thinks this, a road appears in her imagination, directly in front of Coyote, cars flying past. She feels him pause for a moment at the edge of the road, listening to the barking from the other side. Then a squirrel scurries down a nearby tree and runs toward the road. Coyote starts after it, and Charley hurriedly opens her eyes. She doesn't want to see a car coming, hear the squeal of brakes, the thump of a collision. Could this vision be true? Or worse, could the very act of seeing *make* it true?

As the morning drags by, she checks the windows every few minutes to see if he's back. Every so often Charley goes outside to whistle for him. She whistles so loud and so often that Sadie finally comes, and she gives her a biscuit and apologizes for not playing with her. When she goes inside, Sadie stays, lying on the porch so that every time Charley comes to see if Coyote is back her heart jolts when she sees the red-gold form against the sliding doors. Finally she decides to walk Sadie home. Maybe Coyote will find them and join them on the trail.

Everything about the walk this time is wrong. Spiderwebs seem purposely placed to miss the spider stick, catching her bare arms with their sticky filaments. The honking of the goose family grates on her ears, and the usually cheerful chatter call of a kingfisher sounds suddenly harsh and discordant. Even the smell of the lake seems wrong, fishy and unpleasant.

In one place, where the trail drops sharply as it curves around a tree, she grabs the tree for support and puts her hand directly on a thick, hairy poison ivy vine that runs up the trunk. Stupid! The poison ivy has been growing on that tree all summer. She knows to use the sapling on the other side of the trail for support instead, but she's been worrying about where Coyote could have gone instead of paying attention.

Sadie, on the other hand, seems totally unconcerned. She trots this way and that, rushing ahead after a squirrel, coming back to check that Charley's still there, going into the water, shaking and rolling in the leaves to dry herself. Unreasonably, Charley is angry at the dog for being so cheerful when something might have happened to her friend, angry even that Sadie is the one who is here with her when she should be walking with Coyote instead.

Mrs. Davis is outside, weeding the small patch of flowers she has planted along the road where the sun reaches. "I haven't seen him," she says when Charley asks. "But that dog knows these woods better than any of us. He's off on some errand of his own, and he'll be back when he's ready. Thanks for bringing Sadie around."

Charley decides to walk home the long way on the road. She can tell anyone she sees to keep a lookout for Coyote, to call her if they see him. But nobody else is out. She is across the dam and halfway up the road to her house before she sees Mrs. Jensen walking toward her with Bo, her old black dog, moving slowly and steadily along behind, stopping to sniff, stopping to lift his leg unsteadily to pee. "Where's your buddy?" Mrs. Jensen asks Charley.

"I haven't seen him since last night. He hasn't come for his walk or his snacks or anything!"

"Now don't you worry yourself." Mrs. Jensen pats Charley's arm. Bo moves slowly forward, his tail wagging gently, and puts his white muzzle against Charley's hand. Eighteen years old, Bo is the oldest dog Charley has ever heard of. She pats his head. Like Tree, she thinks, Bo is a survivor.

"Bo used to roam, you know," Mrs. Jensen says. "Used to scare me silly when he'd just up and disappear. He'd be gone for a couple of days sometimes, and then, 'bout the time I was thinking we'd lost him for good, he'd come wandering back, grinning and wagging his tail like he'd been on vacation at the shore. Never did know what he was up to. Don't you go fussing yourself about that wild dog of yours, Sweetie. He's just off for a jaunt somewhere."

It is Mrs. Jensen's comforting words that get Charley through the rest of the day. He'll be back for dinner, she tells herself. He'll be back.

At Sarita's urging, she goes swimming with the Davises, taking a swim noodle from the dock box so she can just float, letting the water wash over and around her as she listens to Jeremy and Bethanne dare each other to try greater and greater feats of bravery. "Watch me!" they call to their mother on her inflatable chair as they leap off the raft or put their faces in the water or take hold of Sadie's tail and let her pull them after her through the water. Mrs. Davis raises her glass of wine and toasts their every trick.

"Watch me, watch me!" The words, the whoops and giggles and splashes, take Charley back to summer evenings with her mother and father. She used to show off for them the way the Davis kids are doing now, and then climb, shivering and blue fingered, onto the raft and wrap herself in a towel to get warm before going in again. Her mother, who swam the length of the lake first thing every morning from May to October, never seemed to get cold. She could stay in the water until the fireflies were out.

Charley closes her eyes and feels the lap of the water, cool against her chin. Memories fill her mind—full-moon nights when the sun would go down behind the hills at the shallow end of the lake just a little while before the golden globe of the moon rose over the hills down toward the dam. The three of them would sit on the raft, the canoe tied the way it is this moment, watching the moon spill a pathway of silver onto the water. She can hear her parents' voices, the sound of her father laughing. The plane crash, Charley thinks, didn't just take her mother from her. It took her father, that man laughing on the swim dock in the moonlight, too.

A dog begins to bark, and Charley opens her eyes with a start. It is not Coyote's bark. Mrs. Sutcliff, wearing sunglasses and a baseball cap, an orange swim noodle sticking into the air on either side, is swimming down the lake toward them. Her chocolate Lab, Boone, is swimming in front of her, barking at Sadie, who is splashing toward him now, her tail flinging water as she goes. Charley glances at the empty place onshore where Coyote ought to be. The chill settles into the space beneath her ribs again.

Coyote does not show up for his meal. Her father and Sarita try to reassure her at dinner. "Just think how long he went without eating before," her father says. His words don't help. Nearly starving should have made Coyote more focused than other dogs on where and when he's fed.

A couple of days, Charley reminds herself as she turns on the porch and ramp lights when it gets dark. Mrs.

Jensen said Bo would be gone a couple of days sometimes. But when she goes out at bedtime with liver in her
hand, it is as if the darkness, loud with the sounds of
cicadas and crickets and frogs, and the occasional mut-
tering of the geese from the water, has been emptied of
all life.

24

Four Days

*C*harley is running along a twilight road between tow-
ering trees, chasing a figure she can barely make out
ahead of her. The faster she runs, the smaller it gets, moving
beyond her, dwindling into the distance. The world darkens
around her. She slows then, her footsteps pounding in her ears
like a drum changing rhythm. It is no use. She cannot catch
up. The figure has disappeared now. She stops, doubles over,
and tries to get her breath. When she straightens up again, she
sees that she is at the edge of a lake, a silvery path stretching
across it under the moon. She remembers this path. It will
take her home. She steps out onto the water, moving one foot,
then the other, walking on the glittering light. She is straining
her eyes into the distance, trying to see the other shore, the
lights of her house, when the black spot appears against the

sheen of moonlight. Her bones turn to ice. Already the spot is growing, swallowing light, closing in.

It is the fourth day, and Charley is walking the sewer line trail. Each day since Coyote disappeared, she has wakened after a fitful night punctuated with a new version of her old nightmare, to begin another day of emptiness, another day of walking and whistling and waiting. On the second day she put a notice in the message boxes, asking anyone who sees Coyote to call her. No one has. She and Sarita have driven up and down the county road and through all the housing developments out beyond Eagle Lake, moving up one curving street and down another, asking everyone they encounter if they have seen a golden dog with a green collar. No one has seen him.

Every morning she has written the day's number on her calendar—64, 65, 66. She refuses to let herself think that The Taming could be over. But today, when she put the red 67 in the square for Friday, August 15, she felt the way she felt all those years ago when her father insisted that there were no elves or fairies in the woods. What she wants to believe more than anything in the world is slipping away even as she holds on with every scrap of determination she can muster.

It is a gray day, dark clouds threatening rain, the air

hot and heavy and still. She has walked from her house to Crazy Sherman's and back, and has started up toward Dixie Trace. Her waist pack is full of liver and biscuits just in case. She will walk every trail she knows before she goes back to eat whatever Sarita makes for lunch. She will go to every place she and Coyote have ever been together, every place he has ever returned to her after a ramble, to get his treats. She will whistle and call for him. And she will be careful not to let her imagination loose.

On the second day she tried a different sort of imagining, keeping careful control of the images, picturing only what she wanted to be true—Coyote in the Eagle Lake woods, heading home, a bone he had stolen from a yard in one of the developments between his teeth. But she couldn't hold the image against the thought of roads, of cars and trucks, and a new one—a pack of dogs defending their territory, surrounding him, barking, snarling, growling. Whatever guided her visions before, when she relaxed and let her mind play, now it was fear that took over, making the images, the sensations. She dares not trust herself to try again.

Since then she has done her best to keep her mind focused as completely as possible on the certainty that wherever he is, Coyote is a survivor. Like Bo. Like Tree.

Now, as she moves along the trail, Charley realizes that in the weeks she and Coyote have walked here, the natural world has changed, without her thinking about it, almost without her noticing. Gingerly she takes hold of a blackberry cane, its thorns pricking her fingers, to move it out of her way. It snaps back, catches on her jeans, piercing through to her leg. The brambles are still growing, narrowing the trail, but the berries are long gone. Goldenrod and Queen Anne's lace and thistles are blooming, now, head high in some places. Even on a day like this one, threatening rain, the world seems drier, the greens less green, and here and there a red leaf signals that autumn is on its way. Nothing stays the same, Charley thinks. Everything goes away.

Looking at the goldenrod, growing so thickly, so bright and tall, she finds she can't remember what this trail looked like before it bloomed. Is this why her mother chose photography? Was she trying to catch it all before it went away? Her mother is not here to answer. Will never answer.

Charley stops as if she has run into a wall. What if Coyote doesn't come back? What if the image of the road, the cars, was real, and there is nothing left of him now but a body among the weeds, a reason for the vultures that circle overhead to tilt their wings and drop down to the pavement? She never thought, in all these sixty-seven days, to take a picture of him. How could she—Charley Morgan, daughter of Colleen Morgan, nature photographer—not once think to go to her mother's studio, dig through the boxes, find a camera, and take a picture? If he is gone, there will be nothing to show that Coyote ever lived. Nothing—nothing at all—to show for day after day of the effort to tame him, day after day of their growing connection.

Ahead Charley sees the wild rosebush that marks the way into the Pine Grove. She pushes past it, makes her way through the young pines, and scrambles up the hill. The Pine Grove has changed only a little since the day she found it, she sees. The moss seems taller, the lichens thicker, and a dead branch, with a pair of gray pinecones still attached, lies across the place where the fairy rings grow. She is not comforted. However small, it is change. Charley sinks to the ground, stretches her legs out in front of her, leans against a tree. She tries to settle herself, to breathe slowly, to focus her attention on a bit of moss, an ant, the thrum of cicadas. But she cannot seem to get her breath.

Something that feels like a great balloon in the center of her is growing, pushing against her ribs, against her throat. If it gets any bigger, she thinks she will explode, shattering into so many pieces she will never be able to put herself together again. She tries to swallow around a pain like blackberry thorns, and a sound begins. She hears it before she understands that it is coming from inside herself. A low moan, it grows louder, rises higher, until it becomes a kind of scream, and she is crying, tears flooding her eyes, pouring down her cheeks. She cannot make them stop. There is no way to wake up from this pain, no way to get away. The black spot from her nightmares has swallowed her. Sobbing, Charley throws herself down on the moss.

Memories come flooding in. The day her father turned from the telephone, his face gone gray and old, to say the words that made no sense: "Your mother's plane went down, Charley. Your mother is gone." Neighbors with casseroles. People crowding the house. The funeral at the church that she and her father have never gone back to again. Taking down her mother's photographs, trying not to see them as she did it. Mrs. Jensen coming at her, touching, patting, hugging—the very things Charley did not want, could not stand. Amy—acting so weird, afraid to mention her own mother until the day Charley yelled at her to stop worrying about her, the day she told everybody at school that she was all right. That it was all over, and she didn't hurt anymore. Wouldn't cry anymore.

Other memories come, then, a flood that won't stop. The hospital. Amy and Travis, scraped and bruised but on their feet—"treated and released"—walking so easily into the room, one foot then the other. Travis apologizing. Sorry. Sorry. Sorry. The room full of balloons that she had to lie there and watch shrink and droop, flowers she had to watch die. Cards from the kids at school. "Get well." As if she had the flu, as if when she gets out of the hospital, she can come back to school and everything will be okay. Wheelchair, crutches, Tony. Pain.

Amy's mother on the phone talking about tennis. Becky Sue Lindner and Lake George. Amy gone for the summer with never a word.

And Coyote! A "good thing" she was doing, Dr. Frazier said. She understands now that it hasn't been only her saving Coyote. It has been, since that very first day, Coyote saving her. Coyote gone now, like everything else.

Charley doesn't know how long the sobbing lasts, but when it dwindles, stops, she lies still for a long time, unable to move. She is exhausted, limp, as if the life has been wrung out of her and there is nothing left. Never in her life has she felt so completely alone.

When at last she pushes herself up to a sitting position, her nose is running and there are pine needles stuck to her cheeks. She wipes her face with the bottom of her T-shirt, pulls her legs up and wraps her arms around them, resting her chin on her knees.

Little by little she becomes aware of the sounds around her. Thunder growls in the distance, and she sees that it is darker now than it was. It will rain soon, she thinks. She should go home. But she doesn't move. She is breathing and counting now, long, slow breaths that don't fill the emptiness inside.

She closes her eyes, listens. And becomes aware of her heart, quiet and steady, a slow beat that blends into the zithering of cicadas and crickets, the shriek of a hawk high above the pines. She is not alone. Time seems to stop or stretch. She feels as if she has slipped out of the world of humans, into a realm entirely separate, of other beings—trees and birds, mushrooms and insects and stones.

Something moves nearby, and Charley opens her eyes. Into the dim corridor between trees to her left steps a fox. She holds her breath. It has not seen her. It stands for a moment, utterly still, and then sits, black ears up, cinnamon coat fairly glowing in the shadows, and wraps its brush of a tail around delicate white feet.

She thinks it may be the most beautiful thing she has ever seen, bright and astonishingly clean, as if it is a plush toy, newly made. Its tail is stunning, each hair shading from cinnamon to gold, to brown, to black. There is a rustle in the pine needles behind Charley, and she turns her head toward the sound. When she turns back, the fox is gone.

Like a ghost, she thinks. Like Coyote.

Coyote. *Come back. Come home!* She sends these thoughts into the air around her, beaming the message out to wherever Coyote might be. *Come home!*

And then, quite clearly, she knows that he is not a body among the weeds somewhere. This is no imagining. She is sure of it. She feels the steady pulse of his heart as surely as she feels her own.

25

Home

By the time Charley gets home, it is raining hard, lightning flashing, thunder rolling closer, the trees leaning in the wind. Her hair is plastered to her scalp, sodden clothes cling to her skin, and her teeth are chattering.

She is halfway up the ramp when the sliding door opens, and Sarita tosses her a beach towel. "It's about time you got back, girl! Look at you, soaked to the skin. Get those muddy boots off before you come in," she says. But there is something in her voice that doesn't match the gruffness of her words.

When Charley has loosened her boots, pulled them off, stepped into the dining room, she sees that Sarita is beaming. This tall, thin woman Charley has thought immovable as a wood carving seems lit from within.

"What?"

"Mr. Heyward called," Sarita says. "He has a friend who lives over by the high school who has a young female malamute he wants to breed someday. She came into heat for the first time last week, and for days there have been dogs hanging around his yard. One of them is gold—with a green collar."

Charley remembers her first imagining—Coyote weaving through trees toward the sound of barking dogs.

"They've been barking and howling all night, so the man's wife finally made him take the malamute to a kennel this morning."

Charley puts her hand against her chest, where her heart is thudding almost painfully. "The high school's so far!" *Roads and cars. He could not have gotten there without roads and cars.* "We have to go get him."

"No telling where he is by now."

Even if they found him, Charley realizes, she can't be sure he would come to her, can't be sure she could get him in the car.

"You have to let him come home on his own," Sarita says.

He's a survivor, Charley reminds herself. If he got there, he can get back. "Will he? Will he come home?"

"What do you think?"

Charley considers for a moment and then nods. The connection between them is real. She knows this. She makes an image of him in her mind, far from roads and cars, heading home. *Be careful!* she thinks.

"Now go get into some dry clothes and then call Mr. Heyward and thank him."

It is dusk when Charley, going to the window for what feels like the millionth time, sees Coyote coming down the road from the direction of Mr. Garrison's. He is wet and muddy, tail down, ears tipped sideways against the rain that has kept up steadily all day. "Dad! Sarita!" she shrieks. "He's here. He's back!" She opens the sliding door and calls to him. "Coyote, dinner! Come get your dinner!"

He is limping slightly as he trots down the driveway, but otherwise, she thinks, he is himself. There is something jaunty in the way he moves, something cheerful and casual and ordinary. As if he has only been off on a ramble and is, of course, coming home for his dinner.

Charley hurries to the kitchen, puts all the pieces of liver she has into the bowl she has kept ready since she filled it with dry food the day he disappeared. When she carries it into the dining room, Coyote is standing on the ramp under the roof overhang. He shakes himself, splashing muddy water on the bricks, on the glass of the door. "You're gonna like this!" she tells him as she puts the bowl down.

He wags his sodden tail and looks up at her expectantly. He has been without food for four days, she thinks, and this food smells of liver. But he does not move toward it. *I can't eat, you know, until you back away from the bowl.*

"Don't you ever, ever do that again!" she says, and steps back into the house. Sarita is watching from the doorway to the kitchen.

Paul Morgan has come into the dining room. He puts a hand on Charley's shoulder and they stand, watching Coyote eat. "No way to hold him to that, you know."

When Coyote has finished his meal, has settled himself behind the boxwoods to sleep, Charley goes downstairs. She opens the door to the studio and turns on the light. Her mother took her favorite cameras with her to the rainforest, of course. They were lost in the crash. But somewhere here, with her old equipment, there will be the digital camera she got and hardly used before she went away.

Colleen Morgan hadn't wanted to work with a digital camera. Hadn't wanted to let computers take over her world. But she didn't intend to be left behind, either.

"The world has changed," Charley remembers her saying as she pulled the new camera from its box, took out the manual, the batteries, the memory card. "I'll keep doing things my way, too, but I have to know what this new way has to offer."

That is the camera Charley intends to find. She will take pictures of Coyote tomorrow. She will make a disk of the pictures for school on Monday. When the other kids ask about the accident, about how she is now, how it feels to come back to school after so long away, she will have something else to talk about and something to show them. If a teacher asks her to write about her summer, she will create an illustrated report. She will call it "Coyote Summer," and she will get an A.

Charley finds the camera in the second carton she opens. It has been packed away in its original box. Beneath this box, wrapped in bubble wrap, is one of her mother's old cameras. Maybe, she thinks, I will learn to use that one someday. She looks at the door to her mother's darkroom, the sign hanging crooked from its nail. Maybe I'll learn about darkrooms and the way you did the work you did. But for now I'm going to make pictures this way.

She notices the stack of books on the desk. All this time she has been sleeping in the studio, she has not noticed or thought about those books. Something should be done with them, she thinks. Whatever her mother wanted her photographs to accomplish, these books are wasted sitting down here in the dark. She takes two copies, tucks them under her arm. One she will put on the coffee table in the living room where it belongs. Maybe her father has forgotten it. Maybe he will want to remember. The other she will give to Sarita.

At the door, before she switches off the light, Charley looks back at the studio, at the framed photographs that are leaning against the leg of the table. She isn't ready to put them up in her room, she thinks. But someday she'll wake up in the morning in her own room, with Coyote asleep on the floor next to her bed, and see the fairy castle across the room. Someday she'll imagine again the little figure with iridescent wings.

26

Sixty-nine Days

It is the afternoon of Day Sixty-nine. Sunday. The last day of the summer vacation. School starts tomorrow, and Amy is home.

She called yesterday and Charley talked to her, survived hearing her voice. She found herself laughing at Amy's stories about Becky Sue's crush on Adam. But she couldn't bring herself to invite Amy over, invite her to meet Coyote. "He'll just run into the woods and hide, the way he always does with strangers," she explained. It is odd to think that Amy is a stranger to Coyote and probably will be for a long time. Odd and somehow satisfying, too. Charley has taken picture after picture of Coyote, a few of them pretty good. Amy will see him for the first time on a computer screen tomorrow, just like all the other kids.

Charley has planned how to handle school and Coyote's taming. She will get up early every day and take Coyote for his walk before school, then come home and take him for a boat walk. She is not so sure how she will handle school herself. She hopes it will all work as easily as talking to Amy on the phone, hopes old patterns will just fall into place all by themselves.

Sarita is at the card table, working on the newest puzzle, a painting of a canal in Venice. Charley watches her leaning over the table, one knee on a chair, the other foot on the floor, one-legged, like a heron. What, she wonders, is so wonderful about jigsaw puzzles? It occurs to her that she has never thought of asking, as she never thought of asking her mother why she took pictures. "How come you're always doing puzzles?"

Sarita shrugs but doesn't look up. "It passes the time."

"There are lots of ways to pass the time," Charley says, going to the table. "Why puzzles?"

Sarita picks up a cookie sheet full of water pieces, sorts through them, and chooses a piece before she answers. "There was always a puzzle going at the home."

"The home?"

Sarita nods. In the puzzle a headless gondolier poles his gondola over a patchwork of tabletop and water.

Charley moves pieces at the edge of the table, looking for the piece with the gondolier's head and hat, waits for her to go on. It is so long before Sarita speaks again that Charley is actually surprised when she does. "I had a son liked motorcycles. Riding in the rain one night he skidded. Went under a truck."

Charley wishes she hadn't asked. She doesn't want to know more.

"He spent four years in a nursing home—in a coma. I worked puzzles, waiting for him to wake up. Got to be a habit."

"Did he wake up?"

"He died. Long time ago now. Guess I'll go on working puzzles till I see him again."

Sarita fits a water piece into place and begins to hum. It is, Charley understands, the end of the conversation. She realizes she is glad, now, that she asked. It changes something to know this about Sarita. Maybe, she thinks, she will ask her other questions from time to time. Now she will find the gondolier's hat.

An hour later Charley is making the CD of the Coyote photos when Coyote begins barking outside. She sets the laptop on the coffee table and goes to the dining room. Her father's car is pulling into the driveway,

Coyote circling it, barking and wagging his tail at the same time, as if he isn't sure whether he's greeting or defending. It seems too soon for her father to be back from the office, too soon for a contract problem big enough to require working on Sunday to have been solved.

She goes outside. Her father is opening his trunk, pulling out a large, obviously heavy carton. Coyote, spooked by the carton, barks a few times and retreats into the trees across the road.

"What's this?" she asks, as her father sets one end of the carton on the driveway.

"A doghouse," he says. "Some assembly required. It'll probably take me a week or two to get it together. Let's hope it doesn't storm again in the meantime."

Charley can't believe her ears. "Doghouse? You bought Coyote a doghouse?"

He nods. "I never saw a more bedraggled-looking mutt than the one who came home from that unrequited love affair. I figured it was about time he had a place of his own to stay when the weather gets bad. Something better than that hole he's dug himself behind the box-woods. It'll be winter eventually. We can't have him outside all day in a Charlotte ice storm." He digs into his pocket, pulls out a round gold disk with a ring through it, and hands it to her. *Coyote*, it says, with their phone number underneath.

Charley grins. "Thank you. I don't think anybody could get near enough to him to read it, though."

"Not yet." Her father drags the carton to the side of the driveway under the dogwood. "This is his place, isn't it? I thought we could put it here."

Coyote has come out of the woods, is standing at the end of the driveway watching them. "It's for you!" she calls to him. "Shelter!"

"You think he'll use it?"

"He's no dummy," Charley says. "He'll figure it out."

Her father chuckles as he leans the carton against the fence. "Let's hope I can. This do-it-yourself stuff isn't my strong suit."

"You can do it. I can help, and if we get into trouble we'll call for Sarita. So," she says, as he strains to open the box, "there wasn't really a contract problem?"

He grins, a grin Charley hasn't seen in a very long time. "There's always a contract problem. Just not one I had to deal with today."

"Are you planning to start this project right now?"

"In a while. I need to change clothes and find some tools. And have a little something cold to drink."

"Then I'm going to take Coyote for a boat walk."

"Suit yourself. Just don't leave me alone with this thing for too long."

Coyote has come down from the trail and is standing chest deep in the water, drinking, a few feet from where Charley has pulled the canoe in beside Tree. She is holding the boat in place with the paddle, her other hand resting on Tree's rough bark. She is glad to be away from the sun beating down on the open water. Glad for the shade of Tree's heavy canopy. "I go to school tomorrow," she says. She is used to speaking to Tree now, the way her mother did, used to the feeling of comfort she gets when she is in his presence. "It'll be weird being back with all the kids." A dragonfly circles her head and flies off, its wings a silvery blur. "There isn't going to be much time to work on The Taming before Coyote has to have his heartworm treatment. You think he'll be okay?"

She doesn't get an answer. But it occurs to her that there is no point thinking about what will happen next. The future is anybody's guess. She never expected to lose her mother, to have an accident, to find a dog. What is important is that Coyote is here with her now. *Stick with this one day.* She can't tell whether it is Tree or herself she is listening to.

"You want some liver?" she asks Coyote.

At the sound of the word, his tail begins to wag. Stepping carefully over submerged branches, he makes his way to the side of the canoe. She gives Tree a farewell pat, takes a piece of liver from her waist pack, and holds it out. "Chew it this time!" she says. "You can't even taste it if you gulp it down." He snatches it and swallows. She sighs. "I guess that's why they call it wolfing your food." She pats his head, rubs behind his ears. He stands still as she does this, his eyes meeting hers, then turns and picks his way back to shore. *I love you!* she thinks. Up the hill a squirrel leaps from a tree to the ground, scuffling leaves, and Coyote is off, leaping over branches and downed trees, barking his high-pitched, squirrel bark.

"I'll be back," she tells Tree and back paddles into deeper water.

I'll be here.

As she paddles along the shore, Charley watches turtles drop off the logs where they have been sunbathing. A kingfisher smacks headfirst into the water and flies up to a tree branch with a small fish wiggling in its beak. A bullfrog thunders from the cove next to Crazy Sherman's house, and a great blue heron lifts itself heavily into the air when Coyote splashes his way through the shallows of Hawk Pond. It lands improbably on top of a pine tree, the branch beneath it bending and swaying under its weight. She should really take the camera when she goes out, she thinks.

Bethanne and Jeremy are on the swim raft with Sadie. "Charley! Come swim!"

"Not today," she says. "I'm helping Dad build a dog-house."

"Coyote's one lucky wild dog," Mrs. Davis calls from her floating chair.

Charley sees that Coyote has come down to his usual place at the shore, is sitting straight and tall as when she first saw him. The afternoon sun seems to set his golden coat afire. Beautiful, she thinks. She will take the pictures to school tomorrow, but no photograph can show the kids who this dog really is.

She paddles toward her dock. "Come on, Coyote," she calls over her shoulder. "Come home and watch us build your house!" When she turns around, he is already in the water, swimming doggedly after her, a glittering V of ripples spreading out behind him. *Lucky*, Charley thinks, *but not so very wild.*

Bizarre indentions
noted on pg. 195 — En
of book.
6.25.18 KM WGRL-